# Lover Man

Also by Geneva Holliday

*Groove*

*Fever*

*Heat*

*Seduction*


WRITING AS BERNICE L. MCFADDEN

*Sugar*

*The Warmest December*

*This Bitter Earth*

*Loving Donovan*

*Camilla's Roses*

*Nowhere Is a Place*

# Lover Man

Geneva Holliday

BROADWAY BOOKS

New York

This book is a work of fiction. Names, characters, businesses, organizations, places, events, and incidents either are the product of the author's imagination or are used fictitiously. Any resemblance to actual persons, living or dead, events or locales is entirely coincidental.

Published in the United States by Broadway Books,
an imprint of The Crown Publishing Group,
a division of Random House, Inc., New York.
www.broadwaybooks.com

BROADWAY BOOKS and its logo, a letter B bisected on the diagonal,
are trademarks of Random House, Inc.

BOOK DESIGN BY AMANDA DEWEY

Library of Congress Cataloging-in-Publication Data
Holliday, Geneva
Lover Man / by Geneva Holliday. — 1st ed.
p. cm.
1. African American women—Fiction. 2. Revenge—Fiction. I. Title.
PS3608.O4847 L68 2009
813'.6—dc22
2008021407
ISBN 978-0-7679-2965-3

PRINTED IN THE UNITED STATES OF AMERICA

1 3 5 7 9 10 8 6 4 2

First Edition

*To Bernice, who held my hand every step of the way.*
*Thank you, girl; I couldn't have done it without you.*

# Lover Man

# april

# 1

Karma sat up in the bed. Pulling her knees up to her chest, she wrapped her arms around her legs and turned her gaze toward the open window. The view, rows and rows of grapevines heavy with next season's stock, was breathtaking. She'd been waking to this beauty for nearly eight months and it never failed to dazzle her.

"Karma? Always up so early, why?" Sergio's sleepy voice floated up to her. "You are an insomniac, yes?" he kidded as he turned over to face her.

Karma peered down into his deep-green eyes. He was a gorgeous hunk of a man and she'd enjoyed the time they'd spent together, but her heart had started longing for home, for New York, so she knew it was time to leave.

Over the past year she'd been living a fairy-tale existence. Who would have ever guessed ugly, fat, buck-toothed Mildred Johnson would transform herself into the beautiful, curvaceous

Karma Jackson and end up living in a Mediterranean villa with a gorgeous Italian wine magnate as a lover?

Certainly not Mildred! And definitely not the people from her past.

"Come to me, darling," Sergio growled sexily as he tossed the silk embroidered duvet back to reveal his perfectly chiseled naked body and swollen member. "I need you," he purred. "We need you," he added as he gently stroked his penis.

Karma grinned in spite of herself. He never seemed to get enough of her.

She turned into him, threw one hand behind his neck, and pulled his face toward hers. She grabbed hold of his penis, giving it a gentle but firm squeeze as she planted a searing kiss on his lips.

"Mi amor," Sergio sighed when their lips parted. "Marry me today, Karma, please," he pleaded before pressing his lips back into hers.

Sergio had proposed exactly twenty-two times, but Karma never really took him seriously, because he never proposed outside of the bedroom. It was always during their lovemaking sessions. And besides, he was a bon vivant and she wanted someone she could call her very own.

Pushing Sergio onto his back, Karma straddled him; grabbing hold of the dark hairs of his chest, she pulled. "Oh, oh," Sergio cried out in ecstasy. He loved it rough.

Karma whispered, "You are a bad boy, Sergio. Very bad."

"I am bad." Sergio's words came out in short blasts. "You must punish me for my naughtiness."

Karma sat up, pulled her arm back and then brought it forward, her open palm landing squarely on Sergio's right cheek.

"Oh God, yes!" Sergio screamed.

Karma smiled and leveled the same assault on the left cheek.

"Please, please," Sergio whimpered as he rubbed the crimson-colored palm prints on his face.

Karma grinned. "Have you had enough?"

Sergio, his eyes wet with tears, looked up at Karma and said, "No, I have been very bad. I need to be taught a lesson."

Reaching across to the nightstand, she pulled the drawer open, revealing a treasure trove of condoms. She'd learned plenty in the Italian countryside. These were amorous, beautiful people who loved wine, food, love, and sex. And not necessarily in that order.

The daughter of an olive farmer had taught her how to use her mouth to fit a condom on a zucchini in exchange for Karma having corn-rolled her hair. And now Karma put that lesson to use. Sergio watched as the condom disappeared behind her lips.

Bending forward, she kissed his two bruised cheeks before covering his neck in kisses. She slithered slowly down his body, her kisses like tiny explosions on his skin. When she reached his cock, she took his testicles in her hand and slowly massaged them. Sergio groaned and grabbed a fistful of her twisted tresses. Pressing her mouth against his jewels, she began to hum "The Star-Spangled Banner." The vibrations reverberated through his body, driving him insane with pleasure; his hips began to writhe and buck. When Sergio began to whimper that he couldn't take much more, Karma worked her magic and slowly slipped the condom onto his penis.

Sergio had her by the shoulders now, urging her upward, but Karma wasn't finished. She began to methodically massage the base of Sergio's dick as she placed one testicle and then the other into her hot mouth.

His voice floated down to her. He was begging, pleading for her to stop. He wanted, he cried, to come inside of her.

"Not this way, mi amor, please not this way!" he wailed, his toes curling as he fought to restrain himself.

Karma acquiesced.

"You're like fire," Sergio moaned as he grabbed hold of her hips and slipped effortlessly inside her.

A firm grip on his shoulders and Karma began to grind, wind, and thrust in a way that she had perfected and was sure she could patent and trademark.

Sergio's eyes rolled back into his head and his mouth hung helplessly open. "Karma, Karma," he called out to her, his face flushed with pleasure.

"Yes, baby, yes," Karma responded as she released his shoulders and brought her hands up to her breasts. She fondled them, rolled her nipples between her fingers and increased the intensity of the grind. The excitement on Sergio's face multiplied and he began to buck more violently beneath her.

Suddenly, Karma was on her back, Sergio looming above her. Karma let out a small giggle of surprise as he parted her legs and eased his face down between them.

His mouth enclosed her engorged clitoris; the warmth and wetness made her squirm with pleasure.

Sergio could eat a mean pussy. He sucked, licked, and nibbled until Karma's back was arched so high into the air she'd thought her spine would snap.

Just as she was reaching her climax, Sergio inserted his middle finger inside of her. Fireworks went off behind Karma's eyes as her juices gushed out onto the silk bed sheet.

Karma was still panting, still trying to regain some sort of composure, when Sergio came to rest alongside her. "Do not drift off, my love, we are only at the beginning . . ."

# 2

She'd been considerate enough to leave a note. And—God help her—the diamond and emerald ring she'd woke one morning to find glittering on the empty pillow beside her. She did take the sapphire and diamond tennis bracelet, the Vuitton luggage set, and all of the designer clothes he'd bought her.

She was homesick in the worst way. In a way Sergio just could not understand. "Karma," he'd say as they sat eating breakfast on the balcony of his villa, "why would you want to leave such a beautiful place?" He swept his arms across the lush countryside. "Puglia is heaven, and that place you call home, New York? That is hell." And on that note he'd viciously stab the melon with his fork.

After some time she just stopped discussing it with him and began planning her departure. Karma knew if she told him that she was leaving, he would throw a fit and probably destroy her passport.

He was a jealous man, which was a blatant contradiction to his lifestyle.

So when Sergio announced he was going to Milan to handle some business, and would stay over a few days in Pisa to see how the renovations on his apartment were going, Karma instantly understood that he would be spending time with his other woman. Carmen something or other.

Carmen had had the audacity to write Karma a letter and have it hand-delivered. The purpose of the communication, she explained, was, first, for Karma to know that she existed and second, that if she had any fantasies of becoming Mrs. Martinelli, she should put those fantasies to rest. Carmen, who apparently had been involved with Sergio for five years, was the only woman who actually had Sergio's heart. Karma and the others were playthings. Whores.

Along with the letter Carmen had included a picture of her and Sergio in a lovers' embrace at a clothing-optional Grecian resort. The digital date on the picture indicated that Sergio and Carmen were together when he'd claimed he was on business in Sicily. Karma hadn't even flinched. She wasn't upset in the least. It was all a game to her anyway. And so she'd scrawled across the picture:

*Fine by me*

and stuffed it back in the same envelope it'd come in.

"Take this back to the woman who sent it," she instructed the messenger, after pressing one hundred euros into his palm.

The young man was bowled over; eyes wide, he turned and rushed off to his waiting bicycle before the stupid American realized her mistake.

Karma chuckled to herself as she pulled the door shut. She knew how much she'd given him. What did she care? It wasn't her money!

Still smiling smugly at her retort, she climbed the marble stairs to the opulent bedroom where the naked pool boy was anxiously awaiting her return.

Yes, Karma was no saint. She had her lovers too.

When the cat's away, the mouse will fuck the pool boy, the cook, and the husband of the high-profile American politician who kept a winter home just next door.

# 3

Geneva wanted to smoke in the worst way. It was three weeks since she'd had her last cigarette, and she'd been getting past the cravings by chewing on strawberry-flavored licorice sticks.

But a licorice stick wasn't going to do her any good right now.

"What did you say?" Geneva's tone was strained. Her husband, Deeka, was all too familiar with that tone and took a cautious step away from his wife and the pot of grits she'd been stirring.

"I said an apartment."

"I heard that part, Deeka. It's the other part I need you to repeat." Geneva's hand squeezed the handle of the pot and her eyes narrowed.

Deeka swallowed hard. "In Brooklyn," he whispered.

"That's what I thought you said," Geneva barked and then lifted the pot from the stove.

"Now . . . now, baby, wait." Deeka threw his hands up over his face.

Geneva stopped; a small smile had crept onto her lips. "Baby"—her tone soft now—"do you really think I'd throw this pot of hot grits on you?"

Deeka peeked out from behind his palms. He never knew with Geneva. He loved her dirty drawers, but when she got mad, she was liable to do anything.

"No, no, of course not." Deeka's response was unsure.

I should, she thought to herself; I should throw these grits all over his pretty-boy face.

"You know how much I hate Brooklyn!" Geneva screamed as she slammed the pot back down onto the burner. "It's the other side of the fucking world!"

Deeka took a cautious step backward. "Baby—"

"Enough with the baby's, Deeka," Geneva huffed, throwing her hands up in the air. "Why can't we buy something around here or up in Harlem?"

"I'm making money, baby—I mean, Geneva, but not that type of money. This place is great, I know if you come see it you'll love it."

Geneva folded her arms like a spoiled child. She'd rather stay in the projects in Manhattan than move to Brooklyn.

Deeka moved toward her, and placed his hands on her shoulders. "Change is good. This place has served us well, but now it's time to move on."

He leaned in and kissed her.

Geneva had no great love for Brooklyn, but more than that she was afraid. She'd been living in the projects her entire life. She knew the people and the people knew her. Now she'd have to start all over again and that scared the hell out of her.

Geneva rolled her eyes. "Don't try to get over with your sweetness," she declared, shrugging him off and turning her attention back to the pot of grits.

Deeka sighed, moved next to her, and playfully bumped his hip against hers. "It's got three bedrooms," he sang, "hardwood floors, a brand-new kitchen with a double oven and six-burner stove . . ."

Geneva stopped stirring the grits. "Go ahead, I'm listening," she said with a smirk.

"High ceilings, recessed lighting, and . . ." Deeka smiled slyly; he'd saved the best for last, "backyard."

Geneva turned and looked at him. "How many people I got to share it with? Forty?"

"Nah, just . . ." Deeka raised his hand and fiddled with the hair on his chin, "just two."

Geneva's eyes popped. "Two people? Ha!" She laughed heartily. "Must be the world's smallest apartment building."

"Nah, I'm serious 'Neva, you only have to share the backyard with two other people."

Geneva waved her hand. "Negro, stop bullshitting me and sit down so you can eat your breakfast."

Geneva opened the cabinet door and reached for a plate. Deeka came up behind her and wrapped his arms around her soft midsection. "I ain't bullshitting you, baby. You only have to share the backyard with me and Charlie."

"Humph," Geneva sounded. "And where are the other tenants going to go?"

"To the park, I guess. I don't care."

Geneva spun around to face her husband. "Okay, enough games. What kind of apartment is this?"

Deeka's face broke into a broad smile. "It's a duplex in a brownstone."

Geneva gave him a hard look. "A duplex?"

"Yeah, duplex. That's two floors!"

A small smile began to creep across Geneva's face. "I ain't never lived nowhere with two whole floors before," she said in her best plantation slave voice. "You s'pose they gots indoor plumbing too?"

Geneva was being mean on purpose.

Deeka's smile slipped. Geneva had hurt his feelings. "You got jokes, huh, Geneva?"

Geneva just smirked at him.

"Yeah, all right, whatever then," Deeka said before he stormed out of the kitchen and into the bedroom, slamming the door behind him.

"Whatever then," Geneva mocked under her breath before screaming, "Charlie, breakfast is ready!"

# 4

Crystal pulled the bedroom window shutters open and was greeted with a pink shower of bougainvillea that had bloomed during the night. Beyond that was the ocean dotted with a variety of boats, sails fluttering in the wind.

It was sailing week in Antigua, leaving Crystal extremely busy. She'd coordinated four weddings for the week. Two on Monday, a third last night, and this afternoon, the mother of them all, which was to take place on a megasize yacht and be attended by two hundred and thirty people.

She was nervous. More nervous than she could ever remember being since she'd started her small wedding planning service. This particular wedding could make or break her business. If the couple loved what she'd done, then she would be recommended to all of their wealthy friends and family. If they were disappointed, her name would be mud, and she wouldn't even be able to plan a birthday party for a five-year-old.

It was barely seven o'clock in the morning and her cell phone was vibrating on the nightstand. "Crystal Atkins, good morning?" she sang.

It was the nervous bride calling. Crystal listened intently as the woman rambled on and on about how everything had to go off without a hitch and how this was the most important day of her life and how she would die . . . JUST DIE . . . if everything wasn't absolutely, positively perfect!

Crystal grinned. They'd been having the same conversation for three straight months.

"Laura," Crystal began, when the bride finally stopped talking long enough to take a breath. "It's all going to be fine. The car will be at your hotel to collect you and your bridal party at exactly eight a.m. When you get to the spa there will be a light breakfast for you and the other girls to enjoy before your treatments begin.

"I spoke to Evan, and he and his groomsmen will be picked up at 8:30, so there will be no chance that the two of you will see each other. I confirmed his tee-off time for 9:15—"

"I just don't know why he feels he needs to play golf on our wedding day!" Laura screamed from her hotel suite at Jumby Bay. She was becoming frantic, but Crystal kept her voice low and her tone calm.

"It relaxes him, Laura, you know that. Now, I'll be at the resort around noon and before you know it, it'll be three o'clock and you'll be Mrs. Rubenstein."

Sometimes Crystal felt more like a therapist than a wedding planner.

They said their goodbyes and Crystal officially began her day.

On tiptoe she crept to the second bedroom to check on her son, Javid.

Javid was in his favorite position, on his knees, bottom stuck up into the air. He was two years old. She didn't know where the time had gone. In her opinion it was going all too fast. It seemed like just yesterday she was carrying him inside of her and now he was walking, talking and feeding himself.

Crystal felt herself becoming soupy with emotion, but quickly shrugged it off and headed toward the front of the house. In the living room she scooped up her laptop before passing through the open sliding glass doors and out onto the veranda.

How many people could claim an outside office with a view of the ocean?

She used the moments the laptop took to boot up to lean back into her cushioned wicker chair and sip her freshly squeezed guava juice.

It was during these moments that she was most aware of her blessings, and after setting the empty glass down onto the table, she offered up a small prayer of thanks to the universe.

An hour later, after responding to a dozen e-mails and sending twice as many, she strolled into Javid's room and began to delicately rouse him.

"Up, up, sleepyhead," Crystal said as she tickled the bottoms of his feet.

Javid rolled onto his back and pressed his small hands over his eyes.

"C'mon now, Javid, you can't sleep your life away."

Javid flipped over, giving her his back.

Crystal sighed. Most days she didn't mind the wake-up game they played every morning. But today, she thought as she glanced at the Mickey Mouse clock on the wall, she just had too much to do.

"Hey, little man, this day determines whether or not Mommy will be able to afford your college tuition in sixteen years, 'cause we know your daddy won't be able to—"

Crystal slapped her hands over her mouth. Where had that come from? She walked to the corner of the room. Had Javid heard that awful remark?

He was a smart boy; he might not completely understand what he heard, but he'd know it wasn't a good thing by her tone.

Crystal pressed her hands tighter to her mouth. No matter how angry Javid's father, Neville, made her (which wasn't often), she never spoke badly about him around Javid. So this slip, which came seemingly from nowhere, went totally against the ideals she'd put in place.

Crystal walked out into the hallway. The air in the bedroom had suddenly become stifling.

"Stop fooling yourself, Crystal, you know where the hell it came from," she whispered to the walls. "It came from the fact that you know that Neville will never take you as his wife. Not in the traditional sense. His words, not mine." Crystal's voice rose and she moved down the hall and into her bedroom.

"You agreed to the arrangement. He didn't force you to have the baby, to move to the island. That was all your idea.

"You knew he was a gigolo and that you would have to share him with dozens of women. Hundreds of women! And now the thought of him touching you makes you sick to your stomach!"

Again, Crystal found her hands over her mouth. She moved to the dresser and her reflection glared at her from the mirror.

"Thought you could handle it. But you can't. Two years you've been smiling and grinning through how many weddings?"

Crystal didn't know.

"You so want to be a bride, to be a wife, to be someone's one and only." Crystal's subconscious pecked at her.

"Neville can't . . . won't give you that one real thing you need."

Crystal dropped down to the bed. Her eyes brimmed with tears. The mirror never lied. And these personal conversations, as ill as they sometimes made her feel, were probably the best mental-health exercise she had.

She'd been quasi-happy for a while now. The only reason she was still in Antigua was that she knew it would be traumatic for both Javid and Neville if she separated them.

But kids are resilient, and what of *her* happiness? What of her heart?

"Mommy." Javid's sleepy voice shattered her reverie. Crystal wiped at her eyes, fixed her face with a sunny expression, and then turned to greet her son.

# 5

Geneva's arms were folded stiffly across her breasts as the realtor led her through the expansive space of the duplex. It was beautiful, and with every room she entered Geneva fell more in love with it.

She refused to make eye contact with Deeka, who watched her from the corner of his eye.

"As you can see," said the realtor, Gloria, a short, dark woman sporting a salt-and-pepper fade, "the owners were impeccable when it came to maintaining the home. All of the moldings are original, not that fake Home Depot stuff, and," she said as she raised her fist and knocked confidentially on the wall, "these walls are plaster and concrete, not like that cheap Sheetrock stuff these builders are working with today."

Deeka smiled.

Geneva didn't know the difference. A wall was a wall, wasn't it?

Geneva felt like she was walking through the pages of *Metropolitan Home*.

"And now," Gloria announced as she finished pointing out the particulars of the granite-countered kitchen, "the garden." And with that she pulled open a simple wooden door that led to the most beautiful backyard Geneva had ever seen.

The expanse of the yard had been fitted with salmon-colored stone pavers and was enclosed by a mahogany fence. In one corner of the yard was a Jacuzzi, in the other a fish pond.

There wasn't an inch of grass, but it wasn't missed; the exotic potted plants more than made up for it.

Geneva felt herself begin to melt. She'd always wanted a backyard.

Deeka and the realtor saw the sparkle that suddenly appeared in Geneva's eyes.

"Yes," Gloria proudly announced. "There aren't many backyard gardens like this in Bedford-Stuyvesant."

They walked into their apartment about an hour before Geneva's seven-year-old daughter, Charlie, arrived home from school.

There hadn't been an ounce of conversation between them. Geneva said she needed to think, and think hard, about this purchase and the potential move to Brooklyn. She'd lived her entire life in Manhattan; she didn't know a damn thing about Brooklyn except what she'd seen on the nightly news and the crude playground songs she and her friends used to sing about the borough.

"Aw, c'mon, Geneva," Deeka had cried in frustration, "you're being childish!"

"Am I?"

Geneva had only been to the borough a handful of times, and

that was to visit her childhood friend Noah. Now Noah didn't live there anymore, so really, what was the sense?

"You would have the same complaint if I suggested Westchester," Deeka accused.

"No, I wouldn't have the *same* complaint," Geneva sneered, "I'd have a different one."

Deeka tossed his arms up in frustration.

"Just leave me alone and let me think, Deeka. Can you do that?" Deeka had obliged, retreating to the bedroom and leaving Geneva to her thoughts in the darkened living room.

"Hi, Mom," Charlie said as she came bursting through the door, coming to rest on the couch beside Geneva.

Deeka came out of the bedroom and leaned against the molding of the doorway. "Hey, baby girl," he greeted her.

"Hey, Deeka." Charlie grinned and then the sunny smile fell from her face. She suddenly realized that she'd walked into something. The apartment was somber, the drapes drawn. Usually Geneva was preparing dinner, the radio volume on high, filling the apartment with the voice of the famous radio personality Wendy Williams cackling about some celebrities' misfortune.

But not today. Today the apartment felt like a funeral home. Charlie almost asked, "Who died?" but instead she said, "What's up?"

"Geneva?" Deeka was waiting for Geneva to make a decision. The realtor had advised that there were three other couples interested in the property, all of whom would be putting in their offers today.

"Geneva?" Deeka pressed.

"Mom?" Charlie was getting scared now.

Geneva sighed. She was the queen of procrastination. In the past she'd missed opportunities with the time she took overthinking them. She looked up at her husband, this young man who always moved heaven and earth to please her; how could she deny him this, when he'd given her everything in his power?

Now, looking down into the face of her daughter, it occurred to her that she was the third-generation project girl—not that it had been a bad place for her or the family before her; in fact, it had served them well—but now she guessed it was time for a change.

She gave Charlie's ponytail a playful tug. "Well, baby girl, it looks like we're going to be moving."

"Yeah!" Deeka screamed, slapping his hands together and rushing over to them.

"Really, Mommy?" Charlie questioned with a bright smile. "Where?"

"Brooklyn," Deeka announced excitedly as he scooped Charlie up and swung her around the room.

june

# 6

Karma wanted to wait until she was settled before she began calling her people to let them know she was back in town.

Not that she had a long list of people to call. Before she became Karma Jackson she'd been Mildred Johnson. Mildred Johnson didn't have but two friends and one of those friends she'd cut off before fleeing the country and becoming the dashing beauty she was now.

Seneca, her oldest and only friend for many years, was still living in the Crown Heights section of Brooklyn. She knew this because the information age had made it difficult for people to hide. And besides, Seneca had a MySpace and a Yahoo 360° page where she not only blogged about her day-to-day experiences, but provided her cell phone number where men could be sure to contact her if they were looking for a good time.

Geneva, a newer friend, was the only person Karma had re-mained in constant contact with since leaving the country, and not even she knew that Karma had been back in the country for three months.

It was hard, hitting the job market again after so much time off. Karma had grown used to going to sleep when she felt like it and waking up when she felt like it. It wasn't going to be easy to live by some corporation's schedule. Even though she had a good amount of money in an offshore bank account in the Cayman Islands, she knew it wouldn't last forever, and besides, she needed to get out in the world and down to the business of finding a husband.

How hard could it be, she asked herself, especially since she now had all of the requirements. Karma had always been smart and well read. Now she was well traveled and gorgeous and, to top it off, a firecracker in bed. Shit, she'd seen the Superhead video and realized that that Karrine girl didn't have a thing on her!

Karma knew that SHE was the entire package, the kit'n'kaboodle and the be-all and end-all!

On her arrival back in the country she had had no place to go and so was forced to stay at a hotel. Of course she could have chosen a less expensive property, but she'd grown used to extravagance and so booked a two-week stay at the Pierre Hotel.

Karma spent an entire day in Saks Fifth Avenue, shopping for new corporate attire. In the end, she'd dropped a cool ten thousand dollars. A drop in the bucket for Karma.

She made an appointment with a head hunter, explaining that she had been a personal assistant to a very famous politician (namely, the one she was screwing when Sergio was away) and that she had no doubt that he would give her a glowing recommendation—which of course he did.

Within a week, she had a position with Lieberman and Lieberman, a company that handled hedge fund accounts. Her office skills were magnificent, but she knew that her good looks, sex appeal, and bubbly personality had played a large part in her getting the job as well.

Karma did little more than sit at her desk and look pretty, which she could stomach for 100K a year and quarterly bonuses that nearly added up to another 100K.

The apartment she found was a converted carriage house on St. Felix Street in the Fort Greene section of Brooklyn. It was a sunny, spacious one bedroom and just three blocks from the train station and the bustling Fulton Street shopping area.

After Ethan Allen delivered the last piece of furniture, an oversize cushy brocade sofa, Karma felt like she was ready to let Geneva and Seneca know she was back.

Reaching for her cell phone, she took a deep breath and dialed the first number.

# 7

"Hey, Geneva girl, how are you?"

Geneva pressed the phone closer to her ear. She was having a hard time hearing her friend Noah. "I can hardly hear you. Hello? Hello?"

"Yes, I'm still here, but the connection is horrible. Maybe you should hang up and call back."

"Maybe you should just use the teleconference camera on the computer," Deeka slung at her as he wrapped two bowls in newspaper and set them in the box. "Our long-distance bill is out of hand."

Geneva shot him an annoyed look before returning to her conversation. "Noah?"

"Yes, Geneva, I'm still here."

"So I just wanted you to know that Deeka and I have bought a place in your old neighborhood."

Geneva had superstitious ways and so had held off telling her friends anything about the duplex until she and Deeka had closed and had keys in hand.

Noah laughed. "This connection must be worse that I thought 'cause I thought I heard you say you bought a place in my *old* neighborhood."

"I did. We bought a duplex!"

The line was silent for a moment.

"You mean my old neighborhood St. Albans, Queens, where I lived with my mother until I came out of the closet, right?"

Noah had just skipped over the fact that Geneva was now a homeowner. That was so like him!

"No, silly," Geneva quipped. "I mean Brooklyn."

Again silence.

"Noah?"

"Zahn, listen to this mess here, Geneva is moving to Brooklyn!" Noah screeched to his lover. "Girl, I never thought I'd see the day." He laughed. "Deeka must have slapped you good and hard with his dick! Am I right or am I—"

"Shut up, Noah. I'm sorry I mentioned it."

Noah ignored Geneva. He was on a roll now. "You see, that's the way the universe works, girl. You said you'd never, ever . . . evereverenever . . . move to Brooklyn, and I said I'd never sleep with a woman and look what happened—"

"I said," Geneva said between clenched teeth, "shut up, Noah."

"I'm just saying, never say never," he laughed. "I'll be there in a few weeks, so I can rub your face in it all live and in person like—"

*Beep.*

Saved by call waiting, Geneva thought to herself as she happily announced that she had another call and quickly switched over without a goodbye.

"Hello?"

"Hey, Ms. Married Lady!"

"Hey yourself, Ms. Island Girl!" Geneva screamed. She and Crystal had been playing phone tag for two months straight.

"How you been?"

"Well, good and something else."

"What? Ohhh, girl, you pregnant?" Crystal squealed.

"No, and please don't say that too loud. Deeka's been harassing me for a baby, but I'm just not ready."

"Well, girl, you know you ain't getting any younger and—"

"And what? You're older than me—"

"And I was going to say that you did marry a younger man. A much, much younger man."

What was it, pick on Geneva day?

"I don't need you to remind me of the fact that I married a much, much younger man, my cunt reminds me every day. In fact, she thanks me!"

The two fell out in laughter.

"Gurrrl, you still got a mouth on you, huh?"

"Like that's going to change," Geneva said, still laughing.

"So tell me what your surprise is, this call is costing me a fortune."

"We bought a duplex!"

"Get the hell out of here! No, seriously?"

"Yep!"

"Where?"

"Brooklyn."

Again the silence.

"What Deeka do, slap you with his dick—"

Geneva cringed. "That's the same thing Noah said. Where the hell did you two get that nonsense from anyway?"

"From you. Who else would we have gotten it from? Or maybe you don't remember when you first started screwing him and you were floating on cloud nine, you said, and I'm not even paraphrasing here, that that man can get me to do anything as long as he's got that long, dark, thick dick. Shit, he could even slap me with it and I won't even get mad!"

"You ain't lying!" Geneva screamed into the phone, and the two broke down laughing again.

"Geneva, seriously though, I'm so happy for you!"

"Thank you, girl, but I'm so nervous."

"Yeah, I remember when I bought my place, I was scared to death, but you know it worked out. It always does."

# 8

Geneva was trying not to be upset. She hated to get vexed with Deeka before he got on a plane, but this wasn't at all what she was expecting. He had said that he and the band he managed would be local for at least six months and here they were, barely in the apartment for two weeks, and he'd just announced over dinner that he would be leaving for Europe in three days.

"We still got boxes that need unpacking," Geneva reminded him.

Her son, Tony, was visiting. Tony was the band's drummer, and it was because of him and the band that she and Deeka got together in the first place. Now she gave her son the evil eye.

"Now, Mom," Tony started, raising his hands in defense. "Every time we go on the road, you blame me." He laughed.

Geneva pointed her fork at him. "It's all your fault," she accused in a humorous tone. "If you hadn't brought this man to my home—"

"Stop, 'Neva," Deeka said, snatching the fork from her hand. "You forget I was already clocking you at the diner."

Geneva blushed.

"We were destined to be together," he added, taking her hand in his and bending to kiss it.

"Awwwwww," Charlie and Tony wailed together.

"Hush up," Geneva scolded. "You'll fall in love one day and then you'll see," she said, wagging her finger at Charlie.

"Hey, hey, what about me?"

Geneva looked at her tall, gorgeous son and shook her head in dismay. He'd been in and out of three relationships in the past year and a half. "You, my child, have to learn the difference between lust and love first."

Tony dropped his eyes in mock shame.

Charlie's eyebrows cinched. "What's lust, Mommy?"

*Later that night* after Tony had gone back to his studio apartment in Manhattan and Charlie was tucked safely away in her new pink and white canopy bed, Geneva and Deeka cuddled.

"I hate it when you travel. I miss you so much."

"I miss you too, baby," he said, pulling her closer to him. Geneva could feel his stiff member through the thin material of her nightgown.

Geneva kissed him again. The heat between them never seemed to dwindle. She felt herself go moist. Another kiss and their tongues intertwined. Deeka freed his penis from the confines of his blue and black plaid boxers and Geneva enclosed it in her hands.

They lay there for a while kissing as she slid her hand up and down his engorged member until Deeka hoisted himself up on top of her. "Wait, baby," Geneva said, biting her lower lip. She had something special she wanted to do to him tonight.

"What?" Deeka's face was perplexed.

Geneva was a little embarrassed and she turned her head away from his questioning eyes.

"C'mon, girl, what?"

She had recently become a fan of Shenelody Miller, an erotic novelist whose books were selling in the millions all around the world.

Geneva had discovered her quite by accident when a woman had left her copy of *Pussy Bandits* on the seat beside Geneva in the dentist's office. Geneva could have called her back, but she found the title so captivating that she chose not to.

She was the only person in the waiting area and so nobody saw her slip the book discreetly into her handbag.

On her way home she was so engrossed that she missed her stop on the train. She'd never read someone who wrote so openly and unrestrainedly about the sexual act. And she couldn't remember ever reading something that left her so flushed and more surprisingly wet between the legs.

Now she would do something to Deeka that, before she discovered Shenelody Miller, she probably would never have considered.

"Turn around," she whispered.

Deeka cocked his head to one side; he didn't quite understand. "What?"

"Turn around."

"I don't—"

Geneva sat up and began positioning Deeka the way she needed him to be.

"Geneva, what the—"

"Shhh."

Deeka found himself on all fours, his behind pointed directly in Geneva's face.

Geneva took a deep breath and parted Deeka's tight cheeks.

"Baby, I—"

"Shhhh, I said," Geneva warned, and swatted him playfully on his backside.

Geneva leaned in, took a sniff. It still smelled like ass. Even the peppermint soap couldn't mask that smell. But she knew it was clean. They'd taken a shower together and she'd scrubbed him there herself. Had scrubbed so thoroughly that Deeka had slapped her hand away and said, "I think it's as clean as it's going to get, 'Neva."

Luckily, the bedroom was dark. She might have chickened out if she'd been able to see his brown anus staring her squarely in the eye.

Taking his penis in her hands she began stroking it, long, even strokes from the base to the tip. Deeka happily rocked to and fro on his knees. When Geneva felt that Deeka could get no harder, she took a deep breath and leaned in.

She flicked her tongue, the tip barely brushing the puckered brown skin, but that was enough to cause Deeka to freeze with surprise. Still, Geneva hadn't missed the soft groan that escaped his lips.

Confident now, she slathered his anus with her tongue. Deeka began to quiver and then to all-out shake until his movements became electric. "Oh, Geneva, oh, Geneva," he rapidly chanted.

Geneva's tongue darted in, out and around his anus as she steadily stroked his penis. She could feel the sheet moving beneath her legs as Deeka gathered fistfuls of the fabric, struggling with the mind-bending pleasure she was giving him.

When he could hold back no longer, he raised his head and howled into the darkness before splattering the sheets with his hot seed and collapsing into a quivering, panting mess.

# 9

They were having a family day. The first one in two months. Neville had been in England with his new cash cow, some blond-haired woman with big tits who owned two brothels, one in London and one in Madrid.

For the most part, he'd stopped discussing his work with Crystal. In the beginning she'd seemed cool with what he did and was eager to know the details about his clients. But lately she'd become cold and distant when he happened to stumble upon the subject.

Now they were sitting on the beach, watching their son, Javid, run to and from the water's edge. There'd been very little conversation between them, and Neville suspected Crystal had something serious on her mind.

"Hey," he said as he playfully slapped at Crystal's hand. "A penny for your thoughts."

Crystal briefly pulled her eyes away from her son, allowing

them to rest on Neville's face. Gosh, she thought, Javid looked so much like him.

"Nothing," she mumbled, turning her attention back to Javid.

Neville picked up a handful of sand and then allowed it to sift slowly from inside his clenched palm. "It's something, I can tell. Since when did we start keeping secrets from each other?"

Crystal sighed. She wanted so much to tell him about her plans to leave the island and take Javid with her, but she just couldn't find the nerve to.

Her heart had grown hard against Neville and it wasn't his fault. It was all Crystal and the new man in her life.

A. Claude Justine.

The man she'd met at the Laura and Daniel Rubenstein wedding. It was crazy, the feelings she had developed for this man in such a short period of time.

The weatherman had called for thunderstorms late in the afternoon, which was the exact time the Rubenstein wedding was supposed to begin. Crystal had said a special prayer asking God to hold off the rain at least until after the bride and groom had said their "I do's."

When Crystal arrived at Laura's hotel suite at the Jumby Bay Resort, she could immediately tell from the strained look on Laura's face that she'd heard the weather report as well.

Laura's face was a mix of dismay and disappointment as her blue eyes swung from Crystal's face to the cloudless sky on the opposite side of the sliding glass doors.

Crystal was tempted to yank the curtains shut, but instead she grabbed the anxious bride by her wrists, looked straight into her eyes, and said: "God and I had a talk this morning, and he has assured me that everything is going to be lovely."

It took a moment, but the anxious expression on Laura's face began to fade. "Really?" she whispered in a small voice.

Crystal had nodded her head and given her a confident smile.

In the end, the storm that was headed their way fizzled out over the island of St. Vincent.

Crystal, who was standing on the deck of the yacht watching the sky for storm clouds, received the good news from the first mate. She thanked the young man and then tilted her head toward the heavens once again and whispered, "Thanks, God, I owe you one."

"Who are you talking to?" A silky voice floated to her from her left. Crystal turned around and came face to face with a tall, creamy colored brother with hazel eyes.

Her own eyes popped with surprise. She'd noticed the gentleman earlier, not just because he was tall and gorgeous and was sporting a powder-blue linen suit (not many men could pull that off), but also because his date was a little girl who looked just like him.

"Oh." Crystal smiled and then pointed to the aqua-colored sky. "God."

The gentleman cast a brief glance at the sky, but it was clear where he preferred to look. His gaze was penetrating, and Crystal felt herself begin to blush.

"A. Claude Justine," he said, offering his hand. Crystal couldn't help but notice the perfectly manicured fingernails and how beautifully the heavy gold link bracelet sparkled against his wrist.

She took his hand in hers. "Crystal Atkins. What does the A stand for?"

"Oh," he murmured as he took her hand in his. "That is something I only share with people I feel that I can place my life in their hands and know that they won't disappoint me."

What a line! Crystal thought to herself as she repressed the urge to roll her eyes.

"So are you called CJ for short?"

Claude made a face. "CJ is a player's name, a womanizer." He laughed. "Everything I'm not."

Crystal didn't know how to take that. So she said nothing.

"Crystal Atkins, it's a pleasure to meet you," he continued, and then bent and pressed the softest kiss onto the back of her hand.

Crystal was instantly intrigued. "Same here." She beamed.

He was just staring at her. It was certainly flattering, but it was also making her nervous.

"I—"

"So—"

They'd both started to speak at the same time. "I'm sorry, please, you were saying?" Claude said.

Crystal cleared her throat. "I was going to ask you where your adorable date was?"

Claude smiled proudly, giving Crystal an unobstructed view of his teeth, which were straight and even. Crystal was a sucker for beautiful teeth.

"Yes, my princess," he said, looking off into the reception area. "My daughter, Kayla. She's three and a half years old."

"She's gorgeous and such a little lady."

"Thank you. Do you have any children?"

"Yes, one son. Javid. He's two years old."

"Javid . . ." Claude mused. "Powerful name."

"I've never heard it described that way before. Thank you."

"Do you and your husband plan on having any more children?"

Crystal cast a thoughtful look at her hands. "No . . ." Her words faded into the air.

"I'm sorry. I didn't mean to pry."

"Oh no," Crystal said, her voice regaining its spark. "Javid . . . his father . . . Neville. Well, we're not married."

Crystal didn't know why she suddenly felt ashamed.

"Well, hell." Claude laughed. "It's not the dark ages anymore."

Crystal grinned. "Yeah, thank goodness for that."

"Plenty of women choose single parenthood."

Crystal nodded her head in agreement. "So how about you? Is Kayla your only child?"

"Yes she is."

"And you and your wife want more children?"

Claude's face turned a little sad. "My wife died during childbirth."

Crystal's heart fell into her stomach. "Oh my goodness, Claude, I'm so sorry—"

"Please, please," he said, taking Crystal's hand in his again. "Don't be. God had a plan. I can't say that I quite understand it, but what am I to do?"

Crystal wanted to wrap her arms around him and make the hurt go away. But instead, she placed her free hand over his and said, "That he does. That he does."

They spent the rest of the evening talking. It was refreshing in a way she couldn't explain. She and Neville always had great conversations, but because he'd moved from the U.S.A. at such a young age, there were certain aspects of American life he'd missed.

Claude had grown up in the Crown Heights section of Brooklyn and had played and misbehaved in some of the same places Crystal had.

They laughed and laughed about the ever-present Original Gangster who could always be found at the Red Parrot dance club on Friday nights, dressed in his red and orange Super Fly suit, complete with platform shoes and felt hat.

And the nights spent roaming the streets of Greenwich Village and people-watching in Washington Square Park.

At one point in the conversation Claude had stopped and looked deep into Crystal's eyes and said, "Gosh, girl, we probably crossed paths with each other a million times and it took all of these years and an island wedding for us to meet!"

"It's like that sometimes." Crystal grinned.

She found out that he was in business for himself. What business, she still wasn't quite clear on, but it seemed he bought and sold stock, real estate, and small companies.

They danced to old-school hits like "Flashlight" and "Love Is the Message." Laughed their way through two versions of the Electric Slide and briefly joined a conga line before Claude looked at his watch and said, "Crystal, this is the most fun I've had in a long, long time, but I have an early flight tomorrow and," he said, pointing toward Kayla, who was fast asleep with her head resting on a table, "I have to get the princess to bed."

Crystal felt deflated. She wished the night could go on and on. "Of course, I understand."

She didn't have anyone to rush home to. Javid was staying the night with his father.

"I would love to keep in touch," Claude said, pulling his Black-Berry from his jacket pocket.

Crystal wanted to see him again too, not that she thought that would happen in the near future. After all, she lived in Antigua and he lived in New Jersey.

She rattled off her home and cell number as well as her e-mail address. "It was a pleasure," Claude said before he leaned over and planted a gentle kiss on her cheek.

"Same here," she said, and as a second thought wrapped her arms around his back, giving him a tight embrace.

For two weeks she thought about Claude day and night, replaying every word, every breath, every time he'd touched her hand, shoulder, or waist. That's all she had to live on because she hadn't heard a word. Not a call, text or e-mail.

So on the fourteenth day she decided she would not allow herself to have one more thought about him and wrote his name on a piece of paper, crumbled it, dropped it into the toilet and flushed him, that night and those feelings away.

Just as she was walking out of the bathroom, her cell began to vibrate. She looked at its glass face and didn't recognize the number. She started to let the call go to voice mail, but then answered, "Hello?"

"Hey, girl!"

Crystal wasn't sure she knew the voice. "H-hello. This is Crystal Atkins, who's this?"

"This is who?"

"Crystal Atkins?"

"Ahh, sorry. Wrong number," the woman said and abruptly hung up.

Shrugging her shoulders, Crystal set the phone down on the kitchen table and opened the refrigerator. It was time to fix some lunch for herself and Javid. She pulled out a bowl of salad and some raw fish that had been marinating since the morning.

The cell phone began to vibrate. Picking it up, she saw that it was the unknown number again. This time she'd ask the woman what number she was dialing, "Hello, it's Crystal Atkins again. What number are you trying to reach?"

"I was trying to reach *this* number, Crystal Atkins, and apparently I've been successful." Claude chuckled from the other end.

Crystal's face broke into a grin and she jumped up and down in the middle of the kitchen. "Claude?"

"The very same."

Crystal balled her fist and punched it triumphantly above her head. "So nice to hear from you," she said in a calm, cool, and collected voice.

"I want to apologize for not calling sooner, but I was in Madrid on business and——"

"Oh, I understand. I've actually been quite busy myself." That was a lie. Her schedule had been wide open, and she and Javid had been spending their days on the beach.

"Well, good for you. Listen, I wanted to know if you were free for dinner tomorrow night?"

Crystal pulled the phone away from her ear, surely she'd heard wrong. "I'm sorry, did you say dinner?"

"Yes, you know that meal that comes at the end of the day? Or do Americans living in Antigua call it something else?"

"But, but——"

"Is that a yes or a no?"

"Yes, I'm free, but I don't understand——"

"A gentleman named Oscar will pick you up, say around five, and please feel free to bring your son, I would love to meet him. Okay, Crystal, I gotta jump. See you tomorrow."

Javid walked into the kitchen ten minutes later to find his mother still standing in the middle of the floor staring at her cell phone.

Claude Justine, thousands of miles away in America, had, over the past few months, been more than attentive. Two calls a day and text messages in between those, just to say hello or wish her a blessed day. A bouquet of exotic flowers delivered to her door every Sunday morning, and then there were the letters, long, lovely letters expressing his intense feelings for her.

The letters were her favorite. For her, it was a return to the romantic, something that had been tossed aside in the age of e-mail and text messaging.

Just thinking about him made her swoon. She couldn't imagine how her feelings for Claude would escalate once they'd made love.

Crystal had decided a long time ago that if she was to become involved with another man, she would wait, for as long as possible, before she'd give herself to him. She wanted to be sure. And now she was.

Neville was searching her face, waiting for an answer.

"Really," she said, pulling herself up and brushing at the sand that clung to the back of her legs. "It's nothing," she reiterated as she started across the sand and toward Javid, who'd moved dangerously close to the water's edge.

# 10

"Did I hear you right?"

"Yep!"

Geneva stared into the computer screen. Crystal grinned back.

"Well, I've got to say when you first mentioned this guy I wasn't sure . . . but I gotta say, girl, you look happy as shit."

Crystal felt herself decompress. Her decision was finally being met with some sort of joy. When she'd advised her mother of her plans, Peyton hadn't seemed too happy with her daughter's decision.

"Something's just not right about passing yourself off from man to man, Crystal."

"But Ma, I—"

"I know, you love him." Peyton had sighed.

"I do love him. But that's not what I was going to say. I was going to say that it's not like that. I'm not passing myself off from man to man."

"Whatever you say, darling. I'm your mother and I'm going to love you regardless. I guess I'll see you and your new gentleman friend when you get back stateside," she'd said before bidding her goodbye.

Thank God, Geneva wasn't coming from the same perspective.

"I am, I am!" Crystal screeched happily.

Geneva leaned back into the leather office chair. "I don't know, girl, don't you think you might be moving a little too fast? Living together is a big step, especially for people who've been dating long distance. I mean, really, Crystal, spending time with one another on a Caribbean island every other weekend and being up in each other's face twenty-four-seven is something altogether different."

"Oh, Geneva, please don't start sounding like my mother," Crystal lamented. "I'm telling you this feels too good to ignore!"

Geneva leaned in again; her face held a wicked smile. "Are you sure you're not in it for the money?"

Crystal would admit she'd questioned herself about it. Claude was very well off and he'd been showering her with gifts from the first date. The very computer she was teleconferencing on with Geneva was a gift from him. He didn't mind her working, but he hoped she'd take some time before jumping back into the job market. "Maybe six months?"

She'd agreed. What was the rush really?

Crystal had come to the conclusion that even without the money, she would want to spend the rest of her life with A. Claude Justine.

"No, Geneva, it's him, not his money."

"Okay, so it's been, what, three months now? I'm assuming you've told Neville."

It was Crystal's turn to lean back into her chair. Yes, she'd told him, and it had been one of the hardest things she'd ever had to do.

Neville revealed that he'd suspected she'd been seeing someone. Her demeanor toward him had changed and their lovemaking had come to a halt.

"In a perfect world our relationship would work," he'd mumbled into her neck as he embraced her. "But this is not a perfect world."

Crystal had bawled like a baby against his chest. She didn't know why she felt so sad, but she did. It was like someone close to her had died. "I love you, Crystal, and I want you to be happy whether it's with me or someone else."

Those very words told her why she felt so sad. Neville was a genuinely good and kind person who loved her unconditionally, and even though he wouldn't admit it, Crystal knew that she and Javid leaving him was tearing him up inside.

"This man, this Claude, is he a good man?" Neville asked after Crystal's waterworks came to an end. She nodded her head yes.

"I would like to meet him, if you don't mind."

"Yes, of course, Neville."

The five of them—Neville, Claude, Kayla, Javid, and herself—came together at Brock's restaurant on the waterfront for brunch. Crystal had been extremely nervous about the gathering, but in the end, the two men had been civil to each other, conversing in low, even tones and actually sharing a few laughs.

"Wow," Geneva mused after Crystal had described the meeting. "At some point you better sit down and write a book about your life." She laughed and then said, "Ooh-ooh, maybe you could send your life story to Shenelody Miller."

"Sha-who?"

"Shenelody Miller, she's this writer that just tells it like it is." Geneva reached for one of the books on the desk and held it up to the screen. "See."

Crystal squinted at the book jacket, which was stark white with one word at its center written in dark red letters.

"Does that say what I think it says, Geneva?"

Geneva flipped the book around and read the title aloud, *"Cunt."*

"Geneva, who the hell titles a book *Cunt?* And furthermore, what kind of mess are you reading these days?"

Geneva's eyes were sparkling. "Girl, you missing out. Shenelody Miller is writing the real deal. Maybe when you get here we can go see her."

"See her? Do you know her, Geneva?"

"I mean, you know, at one of her book signings. She's supposed to be coming to Manhattan, to the Roseland Ballroom."

"Yeah, okay, Geneva, whatever you say. Listen, I've got to go, Javid will be waking up from his nap soon and we've got some errands to run."

"Okay, girl, so I'll see you in two weeks?"

"Two weeks!"

# 11

Karma sat staring at the blinking cursor on her computer screen. She surmised that she'd been staring at it for more than twenty minutes when her private line began to ring.

"Karma Jackson."

"I don't know when I'll get used to that name," Geneva said.

"Well, you better get used to it, because that's who I am now." Karma laughed.

"So how's the job going?"

"I'm bored to tears."

"Not with the money though?"

"No, certainly not with the money. So we still on tonight?"

"Yes, now where's this place again?"

"Bedford and Hancock. Right on the corner."

"Oh, um, okay." Geneva sounded unsure.

"You've been living in Brooklyn for nearly three months and you still don't know your neighborhood?"

"Well, technically, Miss Smarty Pants, Bedford Avenue is not my neighborhood."

"Okay, Geneva, don't get nasty. Just jump in a cab."

"That was my intention. Anyway, did you finally connect with Seneca?"

"Yeah, she was a little wishy-washy on whether or not she was going to show up tonight."

"You two still haven't seen each other?"

"No, every time we set a date—not unlike someone else I know—she cancels."

"I caught that slight. I told you I'm still unpacking and just—"

"Scared to leave your house after dark, I know."

"You don't understand, girl, this Brooklyn!"

"I lived in Brooklyn most of my adult life and never had a problem, Geneva. You really need to stop that nonsense."

"It's not nonsense, girl, this shit is real. These people, these Brooklynites, they can tell when you're not from here and then—"

Karma was laughing. "Stop it, Geneva, you sound like some paranoid old hag! You're killing me. Just stop!"

"Okay, no one believes me."

"See you tonight. Eight o'clock sharp."

Karma hung up the phone and sighed as she looked around her sunny, glass-enclosed office.

The New York skyline was at her back, but she spent most of her day watching the busy traffic of people that scurried up and down the corridor outside her glass cage.

She was one of two black assistants, the rest were what she lovingly referred to as the Beckys. White, Ivy League college degree holders who really had no desire to become the high-powered lawyers, investment bankers, or stockbrokers that their parents had hoped they'd become when they paid those hefty tuition bills.

These girls, these Beckys, were just a notch above the sports and entertainment flunkies that hung around locker rooms and stage-door exits hoping to snag an athlete, actor, or musician for their very own.

The Beckys secured jobs at Fortune 500 companies that had client lists made up of some of the wealthiest people in the world.

If all else failed and they were unable to connect with one of the clients, they jiggled their firm young breasts in the direction of one of the company vice presidents, managing directors, or at the very least one of the promising analysts.

From the talk Karma had heard in the cafeteria, there'd been at least ten employee-to-employee weddings that year alone and it was only June.

Karma's office line began to buzz.

"Arnold Lieberman's office, how can I help?"

"Karma, Arnie here. Listen, cancel all of my appointments, I have a very important client coming in at two and I want to be able to give him my full attention for as long as he needs it."

Karma rolled her eyes. She was due to leave at seven. If this was going to be one of her boss's infamous marathon meetings, she was going to have to call Geneva and Seneca to cancel.

Arnie would want her to be there just in case he needed her for something important, like bringing in a couple of bottles of water just so his client could see what a babe he had for an assistant.

She looked down at the list of specifics Arnie had rattled off to her and for some reason she circled the name of the potential client, twice.

*A.J.*

. . .

"Sorry I'm late," Karma said as she rushed toward Geneva, who was seated at a small table toward the back of the restaurant.

Geneva looked up from her menu and stared blankly at Karma.

"What's wrong with you?" Karma said, jutting her hip out in frustration.

Geneva suddenly snapped to life. "Oh shit!" she said, and then slapped her hands to her mouth. "I didn't know who the hell you were!"

Karma pulled out a chair and sat down. "C'mon now, I sent you like a gazillion pictures of me."

"Yeah." Geneva's voice was filled with wonder. "Via cell phone. And I've got to say they really didn't do you any justice. Girl, you look like Jennifer Hudson, just a few pounds lighter!"

"Well," Karma beamed as she dropped her napkin down into her lap, "thank you."

The two smiled at each other.

"Well, aren't you going to pay me the same compliment?" Geneva said, throwing her hands up in exasperation.

Karma laughed. "You look fabulous, girl, simply fabulous!"

"Thanks," Geneva said, stretching her spine and sliding her hands down the sides of her torso. "I have lost a few pounds."

"Yes, I can see that you have," Karma lied. Geneva actually looked as if she'd put on a few pounds.

"So is your friend coming?"

"I don't know. Let's not worry about her and just order. If she shows, she shows."

Halfway through the appetizer of codfish cakes, Karma looked up and saw Seneca peering through the plate-glass window. "Oh, there she is," she managed to mutter through her full mouth.

Seneca had been waiting outside of the restaurant for nearly ten minutes. From where she stood she could clearly see all of the diners, and no one in there looked like Mildred . . . or Karma, as she was calling herself these days.

Every time they spoke and Seneca asked what the name change was all about, Karma would just say: "When I see you, I'll tell you all about it."

"I know I shouldn't have come," she grumbled to herself before digging into her handbag and pulling out her cell phone. She angrily jabbed at the small buttons until Karma's name popped up on the screen, then she pressed talk.

Inside the restaurant, Karma's cell phone went off. She looked at the screen and gave Geneva a mischievous wink.

"Hey, girl, where are you?"

"I'm standing outside the damn restaurant . . . been here since forever, where the hell are you?"

Karma muffled her laugh. "I'm inside the restaurant."

Karma and Geneva watched as Seneca swung around and double-checked the restaurant's marquee. "Le Turk, right?"

"Yep," Geneva replied.

Seneca then peered through the restaurant window again. "I don't see you, girl, and ain't but eight or ten people in the entire place."

"I see you though."

"C'mon now, is this a joke?"

"No, it's not, you have on a red jump suit and your tits are bigger than I remember them, did you get a boob job?"

Seneca's eyes bulged.

"Hey, girl, I'm right over here," Karma sang gaily into the phone as she raised her hand and waved.

"Get the fu—"

The call suddenly dropped, cutting off Seneca's surprised response.

In three seconds, Seneca was through the door and standing over Karma. She leaned in, their noses millimeters apart. "Mildred, is that really you?"

"No, Seneca," Mildred said, coming to a standing position. "Mildred is dead. I'm Karma." She threw her arms around Seneca's shoulders. "I sure have missed you!"

When they broke their embrace Seneca just stood staring at her. "I don't believe it. I just don't believe it . . . You're . . . you're pretty!"

Karma's eyebrows arched. Pretty, she knew, was an understatement. "Thanks."

"Hi, I'm Geneva," Geneva suddenly spouted.

"Yeah, nice to meet you," Seneca said, without looking in Geneva's direction. She couldn't seem to pull her eyes away from Karma.

"How . . . what . . . ?" Seneca couldn't gather her thoughts long enough to push out an intelligent question.

"It's a long story. Why don't we get you a drink and I'll tell you all about it."

# 12

Crystal and Javid strolled out onto the busy sidewalk outside the international arrivals terminal of JFK airport. Claude rushed toward them, scooping Javid up into his arms and giving them both a tight squeeze. "Welcome home, family!" he said as he took Crystal by the hand and led them toward the waiting limousine.

Once inside, he handed Crystal a glass of champagne and Javid a sippy cup filled with orange juice. They toasted.

"Where's Kayla?"

"Oh, she's home with Elvie."

Elvie was the Dominican nanny whom he'd hired after his wife died.

"Oh," Crystal said as she turned and looked out the window at the passing scenery. Even under the bright summer sun, the New York day seemed a little lackluster.

As if reading her mind, Claude reached over and touched Crystal's knee and said, "I know it's not Antigua."

Crystal nodded her head; she didn't know where the lump in her throat had suddenly come from. She'd been excited the whole plane ride, and the thought of seeing her mother and her friends and being with Claude just added another level of joy. But now that she was there, smack dab in the middle of her new reality, she suddenly felt unsure about the decision she'd committed herself to.

Pulling Javid onto her lap, she pointed out the window toward the colorful kites that bobbed and weaved in the air to the left of the Belt Parkway.

"See Javid? Kites!"

"Kites, kites!" Javid squealed as he happily clapped his hands.

"Look!" he screamed excitedly as the expanse of the Verrazano Bridge loomed before them. "I'm scared, Mommy. Monster?"

"No, Javid." Claude spoke softly. "That's not a monster, that's a bridge."

Javid trembled in Crystal's lap as the limo moved swiftly across the bridge's upper level.

Forty minutes later the car pulled up to a cream-colored Victorian that stood three stories high.

Elvie, the petit, rosy-faced Dominican, met them at the door. Kayla was at her side. "Welcome, Miss Crystal, welcome." She smiled, giving Crystal's hand a hard shake.

"This is Elvie," Claude advised, "she keeps things together here."

"So nice to meet you." Crystal beamed as she stepped into the massive foyer. "Oh my God, this place is huge."

"Yeah, it's nice, but remember it's only temporary."

Crystal nodded her head. Claude had informed her that he had started building his dream house in a town farther south of Plainfield. "We should be out of here in less than a year."

"Come, Javid," Kayla squealed as she took hold of Javid's hand, "let me show you your room."

Crystal was as nervous as a virgin on prom night. She knew she'd been in the bathroom longer than necessary, but she just couldn't bring herself to walk into the room and climb into bed with Claude.

She felt scared to death that she might disappoint him. And what if he disappointed her? She didn't care what the hell the experts said about love, in her book if the sex failed, everything else would follow.

"Crystal, everything okay in there?"

"Yes. I'll be out in a minute."

She looked at herself in the mirror again. Checked her hair and her teeth and hastily blew her breath into her cupped palms. Everything was perfect. She'd even douched and now she smelled springtime fresh down between her legs.

She clicked off the bathroom light and took a hesitant step into the bedroom.

Claude was stretched out on the king-size bed, dressed only in a pair of black and white striped silk boxers. Tea lights twinkled from every flat surface of the room and Luther Vandross serenaded them from the hidden wall speakers.

Claude sat up, swung his legs over the side of the bed, and stared at her. "You look so beautiful."

Crystal dropped her eyes demurely and uttered, "Thank you," in a small voice.

She did look beautiful, decked out in a body-hugging, silver fishtailed silk nightgown.

"Come here," he said, extending his hand.

Crystal floated to him.

He pulled her down beside him. "You know," he started, taking both of her hands into his, "if you want to wait a little longer, I'm willing to do that. I'm willing to wait for as long as you need me to."

Crystal's heart swelled with all the love she had for him. She squeezed his hands. "We've waited long enough."

They kissed passionately, exploring each other's mouths with their tongues. Claude kissed her neck, tickled the inside of her ears with his tongue before gently pushing her backward and down onto the bed.

"Oh, Claude," she moaned, when he'd freed her breasts from the material and took them into his mouth.

Crystal slipped her hand beneath the waistband of his shorts and grabbed hold of his throbbing penis. She felt her breath catch in her throat.

Claude slipped the gown from her body, hurriedly shrugged off his shorts, and straddled her.

She looked down and saw his cock; it was long and thick and it seemed to vibrate with excitement.

Claude covered her body in kisses, dropping ever lower, lower, finally taking hold of the lace edges of her thong between his teeth and slipping it off.

He pleasured her then. Licking her clit like an ice pop until she grabbed his hair and begged him to stop. "I want you inside of me, Claude," she whispered hoarsely.

Claude reached over to the nightstand and retrieved a condom.

He kissed her again, a long languishing kiss that took her breath away, and as he kissed her, he pushed the tip of himself inside of her.

"Oooh, oooh," she moaned, grabbing hold of his shoulders.

He slid in, deeper and deeper still, so deep that Crystal felt that they had become one and the same.

Raising himself up onto his hands, he began to stroke, long even strokes that sent waves of pleasure throughout both of their bodies.

"You like it, you like it?" Claude gasped.

"Yes, yes, yes!"

# 13

Karma strolled into Lola's restaurant. Perching on a stool at the bar, she smiled at her reflection in the mirror. She looked especially nice this evening dressed in a mod-style cream, orange and brown baby-doll dress. She turned her head left and right, causing the diamond-studded platinum hoop earrings she wore to bounce against her cheeks.

After a moment she glanced at her watch. Seneca was late as usual. But she didn't mind, she loved being the center of attention. She'd already garnered a number of approving glances.

"Hello, what can I get for you?" the small, mocha-colored bartender asked.

"Um," Karma mused as her eyes skipped across the dozens of liquor bottles behind the bar. "You know, I'm just going to have a glass of Pouilly-Fuissé."

"Wonderful choice."

Karma nodded. Back when she was homely Mildred Johnson, she didn't know a thing about wine, or much about life. But during the past year as Karma Jackson, she'd been exposed to so many things that she considered herself a treasure trove of culture now.

"Shall I start a tab for you?" the bartender asked as she set the glass of wine down on top of a square napkin.

Karma glanced at her watch again. "Yes, let's do that."

Two sips of wine and the slanted-eyed brother who'd been watching her from his dining table stood and began his approach. Karma watched his reflection in the mirror. He wasn't a bad-looking man, but he had locs, and she didn't really go in for men with locs; that would be too much damn hair in the bed.

"Hello."

Karma pretended to be surprised. "Oh, you startled me. Hello."

"I just had to interrupt my dinner and come over to let you know how beautiful you are."

Karma had heard a variety of pick-up lines. But not one man had ever left his filet mignon to share one.

"Thank you. You're so sweet."

"My name is Augustine. Augustine Barrows." He offered his hand.

"Karma Jackson."

"Karma. What a beautiful name," he said taking her hand and giving it a gentle squeeze.

"Thank you."

Augustine glanced over to the three other men he'd left sitting at the table. "Are you waiting for someone, because I would love to buy you dinner so we can get to know each other."

Karma picked up on his Southern drawl. "South Carolina?" she asked.

"Close." Augustine grinned. "Georgia."

Karma turned and looked at the table. "Thank you for the offer, but there doesn't seem to be room for me and besides it looks as if you're already halfway through your meal."

Augustine shook his head, "No problem. I'd just get an intimate table for two," he said, and his eyes fell down to Karma's breasts. "I'll just have dessert, while you order any ole little thing you want."

Karma waited for his eyes to find hers again, but they seemed to be stuck on her tits.

"Do you want me to take them out so that you can see them better, or do you have X-ray vision?" Her tone was matter-of-fact.

Embarrassed by her directness, Augustine laughed. "Oh, shoot, girl, you can't blame a brother for looking, can you?"

Karma smiled and wiggled her fingers at him. "Go away, little boy. Go on, shoo now," she said, before turning back to her glass of wine.

"You ain't all that, Karma Jackson," Augustine spat. "That's the problem with you black women, ya'll think too much of yourselves."

Karma ignored him and began to hum a little ditty to herself.

"You think you the shit, don't you?" Augustine continued, his voice growing angrier. "If you the shit, why you sitting here alone, like some desperate barfly, huh?"

"I think that's enough."

Both Karma and Augustine looked over to see from whom the command had come. A tall man, who strangely resembled the actor Terrance Howard, stood behind them swirling a glass of whisky on the rocks.

"I think you've handed out one too many insults this evening, don't you?"

Augustine sized the stranger up, and even though they were of the same build and stature, something in the stranger's eyes told Augustine that this would be one fight he wouldn't win.

"Yeah, whatever, man." Augustine waved his hand at him as he walked away.

"Have a good night and don't think about dawdling. I've already paid your bill."

A look of astonishment splattered across Augustine's face and he turned to his friends, who were tossing their napkins down onto the table as they quickly rose from their chairs.

"Let's go, man," one of them said when Augustine began grumbling about not leaving until he was ready to leave.

"Auggie, the brother said that if we stayed the bill was on us."

"So what," Augustine shouted, "we were paying our own way to begin with."

"Yeah, man," the friend pressed, "but I was spending money I shouldn't have been spending anyway. So let's just jet."

Karma was still laughing when the four men scurried from the restaurant.

"I'm glad I was able to make you smile this evening," her rescuer turned to her and said.

"Don't we know each other?"

The man offered his hand. "Yes, we do, I'm CJ."

"That's right," Karma cooed, remembering the handsome client her boss had been all atitter about. "Nice to see you again."

"Same here. So tell me, Ms. Jackson—"

"Please, call me Karma."

"Karma, and this is so totally not a pick-up line, but what is a nice lady like you doing in a lovely place like this, alone?"

Giggling, Karma explained that she was waiting for her always-late girlfriend, Seneca.

"Hmmm, Seneca, another interesting name. Is she as beautiful as you?"

Karma wanted to scream, HELL NO!

But instead she said, "She is a very beautiful woman."

"Wish I could stay around to meet this Seneca, but I've got an appointment in a half-hour. I would, however, like to see you again."

Karma heard the words and suddenly forgot to breathe. Yes, she'd found CJ extremely attractive, but he hadn't given her a second look when he was in the office last week. And so she just thought she wasn't his type. But now it seemed that she'd been wrong.

"I'm not going to give you my card, that's just too cliché. I'll see you on Sunday at Questo's in Soho for brunch. Twelve noon."

Picking a napkin off the bar, he hastily scribbled down the address and handed it to her.

Karma blinked. He hadn't asked if she was free or if she was even interested in seeing him. He just assumed that she would show.

"You're a very beautiful woman," CJ stated as he gently cupped the curve of her jawbone in the palm of his hand. "Intelligent and sexy . . . but are you trustworthy and obedient?"

What the?

Karma didn't know whether she found his brand of cocky confidence revolting or intriguing.

She was stunned speechless and remained that way even after he bid her a good-night, walked out of the restaurant, and climbed into a waiting sedan.

When Seneca bounded in Karma was on her second glass of wine, still trying to untangle what had just happened.

# 14

Crystal watched from the kitchen window as Kayla and Javid took turns going down the slide.

Claude had converted one section of the backyard into a virtual playland for the children. There were swings, a slide, a merry-go-round, monkey bars, his and hers playhouses, and a wading pool.

The other side of the yard, the adult side, was made up of a kidney-shaped pool with Jacuzzi, outdoor bar and kitchen ensemble and fire pit.

Every morning Crystal opened her eyes, it was like falling back into a dream. She'd really hit pay dirt, to quote Geneva.

And she couldn't have asked for a better mate. Claude was a loving man and had been beyond generous with her and Javid.

Their arrangement, none of which she'd shared entirely with her friends, was a little strange.

Claude had explained to her early on that he was a very high-profile businessman and because of that he had to take extreme measures to protect his identity. "There are plenty of wacky people out in the world who wouldn't hesitate to kidnap me and hold me for ransom," he'd said.

At first Crystal had thought he was joking and giggled behind his statement, but then looked up into his face, which was dead serious.

He would not allow himself to be photographed and thought it best that she knew as little as possible about his affairs. "To protect you, Javid, and Kayla of course."

"Of course," Crystal heard herself repeating.

All of the information had been a bit overwhelming for her, and she'd had second thoughts about coming to live with him. He saw the hesitation in her eyes and took her hands in his. "It's all precautionary."

He admitted that he didn't have many friends. "When you have money it's hard to know who you can trust."

"And how do you know you can trust me?" she'd chided him.

He gave her an earnest look. "I could see from the beginning that you were a good and decent person," he said, pulling her close to him, "and besides, I could smell a gold digger a mile away."

They'd laughed.

"I also want you to know that I travel quite a bit," he'd explained. "My business takes me around the globe, sometimes for a week or more."

Crystal swallowed hard. What was the sense of moving in together if they were going to be apart most of the time?

"It'll only be like this for a few more years, just until I have everything in place."

And by everything in place, he meant the required number of zeros in his bank accounts. "And then you won't be able to get rid of me!"

Crystal smiled.

"Do you think you can deal with it?" he'd asked.

Crystal wouldn't know until she tried.

"Yes."

He'd left this morning for Norway. Their lovemaking had been intense. So intense that she was still pulsating down between her thighs.

Giggling to herself, Crystal lifted the teakettle from the stove and poured the hot water over the waiting teabag.

The brass-enclosed clock on the wall told her it was nearly noon. Soon it would be time to feed the kids and put them down for their naps.

She was about to pull the loaf of bread from the breadbox when the front bell chimed. The sound startled her. She'd never heard it before. They hadn't had one visitor or delivery since she'd arrived.

Elvie and Crystal arrived at the door at the same time. "It's okay, Elvie, I've got it," Crystal said. She hadn't yet become accustomed to Elvie doing virtually everything. Noah had teased, "I guess you're just supposed to look pretty?"

She pulled the door open just a crack.

"Yes?"

The woman on the other side of the door was of medium height with a coffee-colored complexion. Crystal couldn't help but stare at her bald head, which seemed to shimmer beneath the hot afternoon sun.

"Hi, I'm Shelly," the woman said brightly. "And I come in peace." She laughed, revealing a silver tin wrapped with a red bow from behind her back.

Claude's words of warning about strangers rang in her ears. Crystal reluctantly opened the door a bit wider.

"Sorry about that," Crystal giggled, "but you just never know."

"Better to be safe than sorry. I live across the street," Shelly said, pointing toward a bi-level brick house, "and thought that I would come over and introduce myself, since Claude was taking forever to do it."

Crystal thought, it's only been a few weeks, what's the rush?

"I saw him leaving this morning and figured I'd just come over and do it myself."

Crystal was starting to get a bad vibe from this woman. Was she just a nosy neighbor? Her own one-woman block watch team? Or worse yet (and Crystal couldn't believe how quickly the jealousy monkey had leaped onto her back), had this Shelly woman and Claude had an affair?

Maybe this Shelly chick wanted to come over and get an up-and-close look-see at her competition?

Crystal eyed the woman. She didn't take Claude for a man with a fondness for bald-headed women. Really, though, what did that have to do with her pussy? Which was probably bald too . . .

Where was all of this coming from?

Crystal shook the crazed thoughts from her head.

Shelley cocked her head to one side. "So do you have a name?"

Crystal barely heard Shelly's question above her own internal ramblings.

"Um, yes," she muttered, finally taking the tin. "Crystal. Crystal Atkins."

"Cookies. Fresh baked," Shelly announced, nodding toward the tin.

"That was very nice of you. Thank you. Thanks for dropping by. I really have to—"

"I see that you have a son. Beautiful boy, what's his name?"

A scene from the movie *Fatal Attraction* flashed through Crystal's mind.

"Javid."

"Nice name. I have a daughter named Amber. She's seventeen. She attends boarding school. I just miss the days when she was small like Kayla and David—"

"Javid," Crystal corrected her. "Listen, Shelly, I left the kids out back and the pool is there and—"

The excuse was a partial lie. Of course Elvie was watching them, but she had to get rid of this woman.

Shelly placed her hand on her chest. "Oh my, yes, we should take this conversation inside," she said, and quickly stepped around Crystal and into the foyer.

It took a moment for the stunned Crystal to realize what had just happened. When she'd finally gathered herself she turned around to see that Shelly was stepping into the great room.

"Wow," Shelly squealed as Crystal hurried behind her. "He's made a lot of changes. It looks really nice. Not at all like a bachelor pad . . ."

Shelly trailed off.

So she'd been in the house before. Had she been in the bedroom too?

Crystal shook the thought from her mind.

"We like it," she said, folding her arms across her chest. "I just made some tea. Would you like—"

"A glass of wine. White if you have it."

This Shelly was something else.

After Crystal made the kids some lunch, she sent them into the family room to watch a Disney cartoon.

"This ain't your everyday patio furniture, now, is it?" Shelly said as she ran her hand over the chocolate-colored rattan frame of the couch. "This looks like living room furniture!"

It did. The patio furniture was actually a sectional couch, an ottoman and two side chairs.

"I guess we've come a long way from the round wood table, four chairs, and green and white umbrella, huh?"

Crystal nodded her head.

Shelly kicked off her flip-flops and propped her feet up on the ottoman. "This here is the life."

Their conversation was mostly about Crystal. Where she was living before moving to Plainfield? How had she and Claude met?

After a while Crystal looked at her watch. Was this woman planning on spending the night?

"Can I have another glass of wine and some more of those scrumptious crackers with that funny-named cheese . . . what was it again?"

"Gouda," Crystal spat out between clenched teeth.

"Yeah, yeah, Gouda. That was some good-ass cheese."

# 15

Karma changed her outfit three times before settling on the pale green halter dress with the bronze-sequined neckline.

She'd lotioned her body with a glittering, softly scented cream that lent a sparkling effect to her skin when she stood in the sun.

Karma had grown to enjoy challenges, something that she had steered clear of as Mildred Jackson, and so after some thought, it seem to make sense to take CJ up on his offer.

Her stomach was a mess of butterflies when she climbed out of the taxi five minutes after the time she was due to meet him. She even thought of walking around the block once, just to make him wait.

But the joke would have been on her, because when she looked up, CJ was on his way out of the restaurant.

"CJ!"

CJ turned around, gave her a stern look, and then looked

down at his watch before stating, "I am a very punctual person and I prefer that the people I deal with be punctual as well."

Karma was struck dumb. Was he serious? She was just five minutes late.

CJ pulled the door to the restaurant open and said, "Shall we?"

She knew that this was where she was supposed to say, "Fuck you and your condescending attitude!" and storm off, but she didn't. She strolled right past CJ and into the devil's lair.

"You look absolutely stunning," he said after she'd eased herself down onto the chair he'd pulled out for her. "And," he added, leaning in and pressing his nose lightly to her neck, "you smell wonderful."

Karma quivered a bit. His touch was electrifying.

"Thank you."

CJ suggested he order for the both of them. "Do you eat meat?"

"Yes, but not pork."

Questo's was a Belgian restaurant, and CJ ordered the entire meal in French. Karma was very impressed and extremely happy with her meal and the company.

"So you say you lived in Italy for a year, how did you enjoy that?"

"I loved it," Karma said, just before taking a sip of her champagne. "The people are very passionate." She gave CJ a seductive wink.

CJ did not miss the hint. He leaned in. "And you, Karma, are you passionate?"

"I've been told that."

CJ smiled. "Maybe one day I can tell you that too?"

"I think I might like that," Karma responded coyly.

"No," CJ said, shaking his finger at her, "I think you might *love* it."

He was sure of himself and quite full of himself. Karma was turned on. She slid her foot up the inside seam of his pants. CJ wagged his finger at her again. "Behave yourself, Ms. Jackson, or I might have to take you over my knee."

"And what would you do once you had me over your knee, CJ?"

CJ reached for the bottle of champagne and tilted it until the bubbles threatened to spill over the top of Karma's glass. "I would run my tongue down the center of your back and lavish it all over your sweet sexy ass."

Karma felt her thong go damp, and CJ didn't miss the fact that her hand was trembling when she reached for the crystal champagne flute.

After a few sips, she cleared her throat and said, " 'Scuse me, I need to go to the restroom."

When Karma rose, CJ stood and didn't sit again until she disappeared around the bend. He smiled smugly to himself. He loved it when a woman unraveled right before his very eyes. He wasn't going to have to put much effort into this one; he knew those panties were already his.

Claude wore two BlackBerries clipped to his waistband. One was for business and the other was for domestic. The domestic began to vibrate.

Unclipping it, he saw that it was his New Jersey home number.

He glanced in the direction of the bathroom. Karma would be returning any moment now, but he'd chance taking the call anyway. "Hello?"

"Claude." Crystal's voice came to him from the other end. "Your neighbor Shelly just left here and . . ."

·  ·  ·

CJ had her by the elbow, gently guiding her toward the taxi he'd flagged down. Karma had had a wonderful time with him, even if he did seem a little distracted once she returned from the ladies' room.

He reached for the door handle and Karma, unable to control herself, suddenly spun around and planted a lingering kiss on his lips. She'd been staring at that succulent mouth for most of the two hours they'd been together and was eager to feel it pressed against her own.

"Wow," CJ murmured when she finally pulled herself away. "That was a nice surprise."

"More in store." Karma gave him a penetrating look as she slid the tip of her index finger along the curve of his jawbone.

"I hope so," Claude said as Karma climbed into the taxi.

"Take care of her," CJ called out to the driver before tapping the top of the cab, and then to Karma, "I'll give you a call in a day or so, beautiful."

Karma beamed. And when the cab pulled away from the curb, she gave herself a tight hug. Was it possible to fall in love after just one date?

Of course it was, she told herself. She was Karma Jackson and proof that anything and everything was possible.

july

# 16

Crystal sent Elvie home early that day and got down to preparing a scrumptious welcome-home meal for Claude.

She was feeling especially happy. Her man was coming home and she'd had a brief conversation with Noah, who'd advised that he would be in New York in the next few weeks, although he hadn't booked a ticket yet. He would, however, keep her informed.

The house was filled with the spicy aromas of stewed snapper and coconut-infused peas and rice.

She'd made a green salad overrun with fresh tomatoes, raisins, cranberries, and chunks of pear.

For the children, she'd baked a small guinea hen and a pan of macaroni and cheese.

"Hey, baby." Claude grabbed her by the waist and whispered in her ear.

Crystal was startled, and the spoon she'd been washing clanged noisily to the bottom of the cast-iron sink.

"You scared me," she said, turning to him and kissing him passionately. "I missed you so much. How was Norway?"

"Work, work and more work! But enough about me, how did you get along?"

"It really wasn't half bad."

She'd actually taken the car out a few times, venturing around her neighborhood and up and down Route 22.

Claude moved to the stove and lifted the lid off one of the pots. "Not only does it smell good, but it looks good."

"Thank you, sir."

"Where are the kids?" Claude asked as he dipped the tip of his index finger into the fish gravy.

"Upstairs . . . Claude!" Crystal shouted and smacked his hand. "That's disgusting. You didn't even wash your hands."

"Sorry." Claude gave her puppy-dog eyes. "I'm going to go change and freshen up."

The children down for the night, Claude and Crystal were lounging on the patio sofa, sharing a bottle of wine and gazing up at the star-filled sky.

"So this Shelly woman, you say she's a writer, huh?"

"Yeah." Claude yawned as he reached for the bottle.

Initially, when Claude had received the call from Crystal, he'd felt his chest go tight and then the anger had rushed through him like a tornado. When Karma came back to the table, he excused himself, went to the back of the restaurant, and placed a call to his attorney. Obviously the bitch had lost her mind and forgotten their arrangement. She needed a strong reminder. The attorney assured him that she would get just that.

That evening Claude didn't know what he was walking into, but apparently Shelly had kept her mouth shut, because Crystal was no wiser.

"So what's with her bald head?"

"I dunno."

"You think she had to shave it? Maybe she had cancer or something?" Crystal mused.

He didn't have that type of luck, Claude thought to himself.

"I don't really know," Claude said dismissively, anxious to move on to another topic.

Crystal smirked. "Really? She seems to know a whole lot about you," she said stiffly.

Claude's head bounced with surprise. "Does she?"

"Doesn't she?"

Claude's heart began to gallop.

"Why, what did she say?"

Crystal shrugged her shoulders. "She said a lot of things . . ." Trailing off, she reached for her wine glass and drank deeply. "One thing I know is, she's been in this house."

"Yeah." Claude laughed and took Crystal's hand into his own. "Before I moved in."

Crystal gave him a confused look.

"She was friends with the previous owners, baby. She hasn't stepped foot in this house since I moved in. We simply have a hello-goodbye relationship, as I do with all of my neighbors."

Crystal felt so stupid. "Oh."

"I told you, Crystal, I lead a very private life. I let very few people in." Claude rose, pulling Crystal up with him. "Besides, baby," he chuckled as he stroked Crystal's mane, "I like a woman with a full head of hair."

It was all about Crystal that night. He joined her in the shower, cupped her breasts, licked and sucked her nipples, and then lowered himself down onto his knees, the spray of water beating down on his shoulders as he made love to her clit. Nibbling it, sucking it, lavishing over her soft pinkness. Crystal was beside herself with pleasure. She had a lethal grip on the showerhead, one leg thrown over Claude's shoulder, and when she finally exploded, the strength behind her orgasm caused her to wrench the pipe out of the wall.

"Shiiit."

The word slithered from her mouth as she sank down to the aqua-colored glass-tile floor of the shower stall.

After they made love and Crystal was fast asleep, Claude slipped from the bed and down to his study. Gently closing the door behind him, he picked up his BlackBerry and pressed speed-dial number 23.

After a few rings, a woman's sleepy voice answered, "H-hello?"

"Have you forgotten about the restraining order I have against you and the agreement you signed, you bald-headed bitch?"

"Claude, I was just—"

"You were just nothing! If you come near my house or my family again I'll drag your black ass into court so fast you won't know what hit you!"

# 17

"Karma? Karma!"

Karma's head snapped up. "Um, yes, Mr. Lieberman?"

Arnold Lieberman was red in the face. "I have been calling you for ten minutes now. Where's your mind at?"

All over CJ, that's where.

"I'm so sorry, Mr. Lieberman," Karma stammered as she began gathering the stray papers that contained the childish heart-shaped doodles around her and CJ's initials.

"I don't pay you to daydream, Karma."

Karma took a deep breath. She'd apologized, what else did he want?

"You're absolutely right, Mr. Lieberman."

Arnold Lieberman glared at her for a moment before he shoved a stack of papers at her. "I need six photocopies of this file, three are to go to me and three are to go to my brother, do you understand?" he ordered in a clipped tone.

Karma's eyebrow rose. He was being especially bitchy this morning, wasn't he?

"Yes, sir, Mr. Lieberman."

Karma decided to do a little shopping on her lunch break, so she strolled down to the South Street Seaport mall. She wasn't a real fan of Victoria's Secret, she was a La Perla girl now, but she was in the mood to buy something slinky and sexy and La Perla would be too much of a hassle to get to and back within an hour.

She was holding a plum-colored scalloped-lace bra in her hand when her phone rang.

She didn't recognize the number and decided not to answer it, but at the last minute changed her mind.

"Karma Jackson."

"Hello, Karma."

She recognized his voice immediately and her tone brightened.

"Well, hello to you."

"Have you been thinking about me?"

Karma blushed. Every second since they'd parted ways.

"Sorta-kinda."

CJ chuckled. "Do you miss me?"

A girlish giggle was her only response.

"Okay, let me put it this way, do you want to see me again?"

Of course she did!

"Sure, why not," Karma managed as nonchalantly as possible.

"What are you wearing?"

Karma bit her bottom lip. "Um, a nutmeg-colored linen pants suit."

"Pants suit? Hiding those lovely legs?"

Karma blushed.

"What else?"

"What else what?"

"What else are you wearing?"

"A white camisole. My diamond stud earrings and—"

"Underneath the suit. What are you wearing beneath the pants suit?" CJ's tone was growing deeper.

Again, Karma found herself giggling like a schoolgirl. She placed the bra back onto the rack and strolled toward the fitting room. "Black lace thong and matching bra," she whispered into the phone.

"Tomorrow," his tone guttural now, "I don't want you to wear any underwear to work."

Karma's neck snapped. Surely he was joking. "What did you say?"

"You heard me," CJ said before sounding a kiss and ending the call.

# 18

It was the strangest thing, Crystal thought to herself as she looked down at the three utility bills she held in her hand.

She'd been there for over a month and Claude had not received one piece of personal mail—just utility bills. Not even catalogues.

She shrugged the thought away and started back toward her study, which was located directly across the hall from Claude's study. The study he kept locked. She'd questioned him about that, not that she wanted to rifle through his stuff, but they were going to be married at some point and she just wasn't comfortable with locked doors between man and wife.

Claude just shook his head in that sweet way he did when he felt she was being foolish and said, "I keep the door locked because my business is highly sensitive and I can't afford the kids getting in there and tampering with anything. It's always been that way, baby, even before you and Javid came to live here."

Well, that did make sense, but still . . .

By late afternoon dark clouds had formed over Plainfield, and soon after an explosive sound of thunder rattled the expensive homes. Crystal felt her heart jump in her chest and then heard the children, who had been upstairs in their separate rooms playing, begin to cry out with fear.

Elvie had gone to the dry cleaners to drop off a few of Claude's suits, leaving Crystal and the children on their own for a while.

"I'm coming, babies, don't worry," Crystal called to them as she took the steps two at a time. She went to Javid first, scooping him out of his captain's bed, and then rushed to Kayla's room.

"It's okay, don't cry," she hushed the children as she went to the window to close the blinds.

The rain was falling in buckets as lightning sliced through the sky, momentarily illuminating the street below. In that instance, Crystal caught sight of a dark figure standing beneath a looming elm tree just off the curb.

Crystal blinked and when the lightning flashed again the figure was gone.

She dropped the blind, shook her head, and told herself that her eyes were playing tricks on her.

"I miss Deeka so much!" Geneva wailed through the phone. "I've been working my vibrator overtime. My poor little clit is starting to feel like a rape victim!"

Crystal was bent over with laughter.

"Stop laughing, it ain't funny. Every time I pull down my panties, even if it's just to use the bathroom, she starts to scream!"

"Geneva, you're killing me!" Crystal squealed, holding her sides.

"It's so bad that I'm afraid to use anything in the house with a motor. For real! I was making some smoothies the other day, turned on the blender, and my clit fainted dead away from fear!"

"You are one sick cookie!"

"I know, girl, I know."

Now that Geneva had her laughing, Crystal was starting to feel better, and the storm as well as the dark figure beneath the tree slowly faded into oblivion.

The storm clouds retreated, allowing the sun to show its luminous face again.

"So when will Deeka be back?"

"Oh, I guess in another three weeks or so."

"Yeah, Claude is off again too."

"Where this time?"

Crystal couldn't quite remember. He traveled so much and to so many different places.

Crystal shrugged her shoulders. "You know, I can't really remember."

"Oh yeah, listen," Geneva started excitedly, "the real reason why I called was to invite you to a book signing."

"Really, whose?"

"Shenelody Miller. Remember I told you about her?"

"Vaguely," Crystal said as she swung the refrigerator door open and peered inside.

"Anyway," Geneva continued breathlessly, "it's this Saturday at two at Roseland."

"The nightclub?"

"Yeah."

"Well, that's an interesting venue."

"You wanna come?"

"I don't know, Geneva. Remind me again, what type of books does she write?"

"The hot and steamy kind!"

# 19

Karma felt like an idiot sitting there in that office without any drawers on. Every time she thought about it, which was every other second, she blushed.

And then every time the phone rang she jumped with anticipation, hoping it was CJ.

"Karma, I'm headed uptown, I may or may not return to the office today. I'll call you," Arnie threw over his shoulder as he hurried from the office.

Now there was just one Lieberman left for her to deal with, Joshua, but he was hardly any trouble at all. In fact, Karma was beginning to think that he was either extremely shy or just plain scared of women. At least he seemed scared of her.

Meek, soft-spoken Joshua barely looked at her when he ventured from his office and into the corridor. Not even when he called her into his office to take a letter. During those times he spoke into his notes, avoiding eye contact with her at all cost.

The phone rang and Karma jumped. "Lieberman and Lieberman, how—"

"Are you wet?"

It was him.

Karma squirmed in her seat. "Well, good morning and how are you?" she ventured, sidestepping the inevitable dirty talk.

"Are you wet?" CJ posed the question again.

Karma didn't know if she liked this game. Maybe the guy was just a straight-up freak. And what was wrong with that? She had a bit of a freaky streak herself.

"Not yet."

A low throaty laugh emanated through the phone. "Touch yourself."

"Are you crazy," Karma hissed, and shot Joshua's office a quick glance. "I am at work, you know."

"Are you chicken?"

"You are crazy."

CJ cleared his throat, and when he spoke again, his tone had changed. "Well, you have a good day."

*Click.*

"Son of a bitch," Karma breathed. "Mother—"

"Karma, can I see you, please." Joshua Lieberman's soft voice floated to her from the intercom.

"Yes, Mr. Lieberman."

Karma strolled into the office and took the seat opposite Joshua's desk.

The brothers were as different as night and day. Arnie was tall, with broad shoulders, a receding hairline, and a mammoth gut. Joshua was just as tall, but athletic in build, with mounds of unruly sandy-colored curls.

"I would like you to take a letter . . . if-if you don't mind," he practically whispered as he stared intently down at his notes.

Karma forced a smile, opened her steno pad and began flipping through the pages in search of a clean page. Joshua watched her from beneath his lowered eyelids.

When she finally found a clean page, she crossed her legs, revealing quite a bit of thigh. Joshua's heart skipped two beats and his mouth went dry.

Ten minutes later she was back at her desk. Her blood was still boiling when she sat down and snatched up her purse. She couldn't go all day without any underwear and so would have to run to Vickie's or down to Century 21 and pick up a pair.

The phone rang.

"Lieberman and Lieberman—"

"Are you wet?"

Karma pulled the phone away from her ear and glared at the earpiece. When she pressed it back she said, "Listen, CJ, I don't know who you think you are but—"

"But when you see me you're going to spread those beautiful legs so I can see up close and personal that luscious cunt of yours?"

Karma was struck speechless. Had he said what she thought he'd said?

And how he'd said it!

She'd never heard *luscious* and *cunt* in the same sentence. And shit, did he just cause her to cream herself right there in the middle of the day?

She could imagine more than feel the wet spot spreading across the linen fabric of her skirt.

Karma parted her legs, gave a hasty look around to make sure she was truly alone and then quickly pushed her hand beneath her skirt.

Her fingers came back glistening.

# 20

The tickets, at thirty dollars a pop, included a two-hour lecture and a signed copy of Shenelody Miller's new book, *Moist*.

Crystal was so not in the mood for this, but she'd promised Geneva and besides, they hadn't really spent much time together since she'd been back in the States.

The line to get into the Roseland Ballroom wrapped clear around the block.

Crystal surveyed the crowd, which was made up mostly of women. There was a sprinkling of men; some looked enthusiastic while others kept their heads lowered in shame as they shuffled behind their women.

Every three feet or so Crystal encountered a posterboard picturing the book and with accolades in bold, black letters.

*"Triumphant!"*
*Essence magazine*

*"Unabashed honesty!"*
New York Post
*"Raw, sexual truth that will leave you dizzy!"*
New York Times

Crystal sighed.

The ballroom was packed and buzzing with excited chatter.

They followed the usher to the twentieth row of seats.

"Aw, man," Geneva complained, "these seats suck! We're so far from the stage. I won't be able to see her."

Crystal half-listened to Geneva's complaining until finally there was a *tap-tap-tap* on the microphone.

"Can I get your attention, please?"

A nut-brown, petite woman with wavy silver hair and slanted eyes smiled out over the crowd.

"Good evening."

"Good evening," the crowd responded in mechanical-sounding unison.

"I am Saraphine Miller, some of you know me as Mama . . ."

Geneva leaned over and whispered in Crystal's ear, "That's Shenelody's mother."

"Yes, I think I got that." Crystal rolled her eyes and whispered back.

"And Shenelody and I are so happy to be here with you to celebrate the kickoff of her sixth book, *Moist!*"

The auditorium broke out in thunderous applause.

Then Saraphine pumped her small hands up into the air before floating them down to her sides again. The crowd quieted.

"I want you to know that it is because of YOU," she exclaimed, extending her arms out toward the crowd, "that Shenelody has already made the *New York Times* Best Sellers List and the book is still two days from hitting the bookstores!"

Once again the crowd broke out in thunderous applause, with most of the audience jumping from their seats and shouting, "Woof, woof, woof!"

"Okay, okay, settle down, queens and kings, settle down," Mama urged with a proud grin on her face.

"Now comes the time that you all have been waiting for." Mama rubbed her hands together. "Please help me welcome my daughter and the writer you made *New York Times* bestselling author for the third time in a row, Madam Shenelody Miller!"

The room exploded in applause. The crowd jumped from their seats and began stomping the floor. The noise was so loud, Crystal pressed her palms against her ears.

Feeling a tapping on her shoulder, she looked up and to her left and her eyes met the menacing ones of a woman with a nose ring and a tattoo of a penis on her cheek. "Stand up and give honor to the Madam," she ordered.

Crystal's eyebrows climbed. Was this woman serious?

"Stand up!" the woman's voice echoed above the clamor.

Crystal shot up from her seat.

"That's better." The woman smiled at her.

The applause went on for nearly five straight minutes, and when Crystal turned to look at Geneva, her eyes were glazed.

This was some cult shit if there ever was one. If they started to pass out cups of Kool-Aid, she was out of there!

"Welcome, my kings and queens," the soft-spoken woman began.

"Oh my God, there she is, there she is!" Geneva squealed as she squirmed left and right to get the best view of Shenelody Miller.

Crystal rubbed her eyes. She was sure now that she needed glasses. First the dark figure under the tree, and now . . . this?

"We've come a long way together. Most of you have been supporting me since my first self-published book, *The Matter Is Dick*."

More applause and shouts of, "I love you, Shenelody!"

Crystal rubbed her eyes. Was it really? "Nah, it couldn't be," she mumbled to herself before poking Geneva in the side.

"Shhh, shhh." Geneva waved her hand at Crystal, her eyes never leaving Shenelody Miller.

Crystal bit her bottom lip. She needed to be sure. "I gotta pee," she hissed into Geneva's ear. A lot of good that did. Geneva was so wrapped up in what the woman was saying she didn't even react. So Crystal turned her attention to the woman with the penis on her face. " 'Scuse me, sister, can I get past, please?"

The woman gave her a sideways glance. "For what?"

Crystal remained humble. "I need to get to the ladies' room."

"Can't it wait? The Madam is speaking."

Crystal swallowed hard as she sized Dick Face up. Nah, there was no way she could beat her, and besides, she was sure that she couldn't count on Geneva to have her back. "No, I can't. I'm about to burst."

Dick Face let out an exasperated sigh and then turned her legs to one side.

"Thank you, sister, thank you."

Crystal pardoned and excused herself past six more people before she stepped out into the aisle, where she was met with a burly female security guard.

"Hold it, ma'am." The security guard had a tight grip on Crystal's shoulder. "You have to remain in the seat you've been assigned."

"Oh yes, of course, I'm just headed to the ladies' room," Crystal said as she tried to wrench herself away from the woman's grip.

"That's at the back of the auditorium and to the left."

Crystal looked longingly at the stage. "Oh, is it?"

The security guard folded her thick arms and glared at Crystal.

"As most of you know, I started writing these books because my heart had been shattered, no, *obliterated* by a no-good, low-down, scum-of-the-earth man!"

The audience applauded. And a few people threw out testimonies:

"*I know that man, girl—I got one just like him!*"

"*We all been there, sister!*"

"*Preach!*"

"It was my way to cleanse myself, to replenish myself—to take back my dignity and my PUSSY!"

The crowd leapt to their feet.

"So I took back my pussy and had to make a decision right then and there as to exactly what type of pussy I had. Did I have thrift-store pussy? Kmart pussy?"

"*I got Nordstrom pussy!*"

"*I got Saks Fifth Avenue pussy!*"

"*I got slap-your-mama pussy!*"

"Once I decided what class of pussy I had, I knew what market I needed to target!"

"*Sure 'nuff, girl!*"

"Ya'll understand that when I use the word *pussy* it represents more than the Eden between our legs, it represents the female mind . . ."

"*Tell that shit, girl!*"

"Some of us spend more time on our Eden than we do on our minds. We're waxing, douching, spritzing, using kegel balls to keep it tight; all that mess . . . all for him.

"We got to start giving that same type of attention to our intellect and our spirituality. Those things will serve your man just as well as your pussy!"

"*Amen!*"

"So many of you sent me letters and e-mails, thanking me for being courageous enough to tell my stories the way I do. And ya'll always want to know when the next book is coming out . . . that makes me feel real good."

"*Your books are like crack, girl!*"

"*When you write a book you don't just put your foot in it, you put in your entire leg!*"

"I wanna thank you for those letters and let you know that it was all of YOU that gave me the courage to continue writing.

"You shared your personal stories with me and told me what you wanted me to write and I did it, because you are my audience and I am your servant!"

Thunderous applause.

"All of these reviews and accolades are not just for me alone, they're for all of us, you and me, we are one!"

At that a few diehard fans rushed the stage screaming like they were falling off a building.

Security caught them by their waists, flung them over their shoulders and carried them to the back of the ballroom.

"I got a lot of haters out there. Including some writers who are jealous of my success. They tear my books and me apart on the Internet.

"They say I can't write, can't tell a good story. They don't invite me to their little conferences; they don't give me any awards.

"But do you think I let that bother me? No way! I get all of the love and respect I need from you my readers!"

The walls of the ballroom shook with applause. Crystal felt it like a heartbeat in the floor beneath her feet.

Crystal, standing at the back of the auditorium, finally unglued herself and walked to the bathroom. She had to admit, this Shenelody woman was a powerful speaker.

That was some kind of power for one woman to have over so many.

She was like the Oprah of sex!

Crystal rubbed her chin. How was she going to get close enough to see if this woman was who Crystal thought she was?

Walking over to the mirror, she saw that her lipstick had faded away. Digging into her purse, her finger came across the ticket stub. A light went off in her head. "Aha!" Crystal snapped her fingers. All she had to do was be patient. Shenelody Miller would be signing copies of her new book, putting her and Crystal on opposite sides of a table, just inches from each other.

They'd been standing on line for nearly an hour and Crystal's feet were beginning to wail. Geneva was all but ignoring her, chatting it up with other Shenelody followers. It was like a massive book club discussion and it seemed as if all the readers knew the novels chapter and verse.

"My favorite was the chapter about rimming," Geneva squealed with delight to Dick Face and a set of middle-aged twins with bosoms so high and plump Crystal wanted to slap the plastic surgeon who had installed them.

"I tried it on my man," twin number one said. "And I got the Lexus I'd been asking for for two years!"

Twin number one slapped palms with twin number two.

"I'm sorry," Crystal interrupted, "did you say rimming?"

Crystal had fond memories of *being* rimmed. But she'd never venture to put *her* tongue in such a foul place.

But these women didn't seem to have a problem with it. In fact, they celebrated it, and Crystal was sure she heard someone a few feet behind her talking about nominating it for a national holiday.

"She's never heard of or read Shenelody," a shamefaced Geneva advised the small circle of women, who in turn looked at Crystal with sympathetic awe.

"Well, I, I've been away," said a suddenly embarrassed Crystal.

"Away where, on the friggin' moon?" Dick Face laughed.

Crystal dropped her eyes.

"So go on, sister." Twin number two turned and addressed Geneva. "You were about to share your story."

"Well," Geneva began with a giggle.


By the end of Geneva's recant, Crystal's mouth hung open in quiet amazement and she and Geneva were just one person away from Shenelody.

"What?" Geneva cried as she turned to dumbstruck Crystal. "Don't act like you've never done it!"

"I haven't!" Crystal cried.

"Hey," the twins chimed, "don't knock it till you've tried it!"


"Miss Miller!" Geneva screamed as she reached across the table and took both of Shenelody's hands into hers. "I just want you to know that you've changed my life and I think you're the best writer ever!"

Shenelody squeezed Geneva's hands. "Thank you so much, queen, I really do appreciate it."

"So it is you!" Crystal shouted, pointing a shaky finger at Shenelody.

Shenelody's face registered a mild look of surprise. "Crystal? Didn't know you were a fan."

Geneva's head swung between Crystal and Shenelody. "I thought you didn't know who she was . . ." Geneva started and then cocked her head to the side. "You two know each other?"

"Yes, we do," Shenelody said coolly and folded her hands beneath her chin. "We're neighbors."

"Neighbors!"

"Yeah, but she said her name was Shelly!" Crystal boomed in an accusatory tone.

Shenelody gave her a smug smile. "Shelly is short for Shenelody."

# 21

*You would have thought* that Geneva had been invited to Denzel Washington's dressing room by the way she was behaving.

Security showed them to the green room, which held three tables heavy with fresh fruits, exotic juices, hors d'oeuvres, and bottles of sparkling water.

Geneva grabbed a plate and dove in. Crystal had no appetite and slumped down onto one of the overstuffed settees.

On the wall was a large plasma screen monitor showing a live feed from the ballroom.

C-SPAN had shown up and was conducting candid interviews with some of the audience members.

There were three vendors at the back of the ballroom selling *Pussy Power* T-shirts, coffee mugs and baseball caps.

Crystal shook her head in amazement. She was actually living next door to a phenomenon.

"You are soooo lucky!" Geneva managed through her stuffed mouth.

"Lucky?"

"Yeah, you live right next door to Shenelody Miller!"

Crystal shrugged her shoulders.

"Why didn't Claude tell you that she lived next door?"

"Honestly," Crystal said with a sigh, "I don't think he knows how famous she is."

"How could he not?"

"Claude is not really interested in his neighbors," Crystal said, but secretly she did think it odd that he *didn't* know.

"She's bald. Did you know that?" Crystal announced suddenly. Her tone was filled with spite and she didn't know why.

Geneva's mouth dropped open for a second. "What?"

"She's bald."

"Get the fuck out of here!" Geneva screamed as she gave Crystal's shoulder a shove.

"I'm serious."

"Queens?"

Saraphine. Mama herself had come to collect them.

"Shenelody will receive you now."

Receive? Crystal didn't know how much more she could take.

They followed Mama down a corridor, dodging dozens of people with Bluetooth headsets as they rushed past them and off to perform some important Shenelody task.

There was a guard standing outside of Shenelody's room. He was tall, wide and menacing. In fact, he could have been Shaq's twin brother.

He instructed Geneva and Crystal to open their pocketbooks, which he quickly rifled through before giving their bodies a quick pat down.

"Hey, hey," Geneva teased, "I ain't had none in a while, brother. I can't be responsible for what I might do if you—"

"Shut up, Geneva," Crystal hissed.

Crystal expected opulence, but the space was small and gray. There was a dressing screen in one corner of the room. In the other corner was a table holding six wig heads.

Crystal shot Geneva the "I told you so" look.

"Shelly?" Mama called.

"Yeah, be right out."

A moment later Shenelody emerged wrapped in a pink terry-cloth robe with matching slippers.

Crystal looked over at Geneva and thought for one moment that she was going to fall to her knees. But luckily Mama eased a chair beneath her and said, "Sit down, baby, before you hurt yourself."

It was all too dramatic for Crystal.

"So, Shenelody," Crystal began, arms folded across her chest. "Funny you didn't mention what it was you did. I mean, I do believe I asked, if I remember correctly."

Shenelody laughed and snatched the curly black wig off her head. Geneva let out a gasp of surprise and slumped backward into the chair.

"Yes, yes, you did, Crystal, and I believe I said I did a little of this and a little of that."

Shenelody gave the wig two hard shakes and then passed it off to her mother. Dragging her hands over the smooth dome, she smiled. "I didn't lie."

Crystal smirked. "Well, why all the secrecy?"

Shenelody sat down at the small makeup table and turned her

attention to her reflection, beginning to remove the fake eye-lashes. "I just don't reveal that part of myself so quickly. You'd be surprised the types of reactions I get from people."

"Like what?" Geneva piped as she dragged her chair closer.

"Well, let's see. Some people think once you've published a book that a Brinks truck has driven up to your house and made a deposit in your cellar. And that's just not the case for a majority of us writers—"

"You don't tell people you're a writer because you think they'll want money?" Crystal asked unbelievingly.

"You'd be surprised," Shenelody said. "Also, when you tell someone you're a writer, all of a sudden they've got a manuscript they've been working on, or better yet, they've got a story you can write for them!" Shenelody waved her hand in the air and chuckled.

"I learned real quick to just keep my mouth shut. Shit, half the time people ask me what it is I do for a living I tell them that I'm a checkout girl at Wal-Mart!"

Crystal laughed in spite of herself. This Shenelody chick didn't seem all that bad.

"I really don't think they believe you. I mean, you're driving a 2008 Mercedes—"

"Honey chile, I don't care if they believe me or not, that's on them. If they want to stay up all night trying to figure out how this bald-headed black woman is sporting a fierce ride on a Wal-Mart salary, let them!"

Geneva floated all the way to the train station. Shenelody had given her three T-shirts, two hats, and four mugs, plus her entire catalogue of books, personally autographed.

Crystal could still hear Geneva's demands:

*"Okay, Shelly. Can I call you Shelly? Okay, Shelly, in this one put 'To my best friend and number one fan' . . ."*

But the pièce de résistance was the invitation to lunch at Shenelody's home. Geneva had almost pissed herself with excitement.

"Did you have a good day, girl?" Crystal asked as they started down the subway steps.

"The best!"

# 22

Karma arrived ten minutes early. She didn't want a repeat of last time. Truth be told, she didn't know why she was even there. He'd been a real dick on the phone, but he'd assured her that he had a big dick. Maybe that's why she was there.

She had a fondness for big dick men. And he was cute. And apparently very well-to-do. The entire package.

Isn't that what women wanted? The entire package?

"Why are you standing outside?"

CJ had caught her musing.

"Just enjoying the scenery," she said.

He bent down and pressed a soft kiss on her cheek before taking her by the hand. "Shall we?"

"Yes."

Karma turned toward the restaurant door, but CJ was moving in the opposite direction.

"Hey," Karma wailed, "where are we going?"

"It's a surprise."

She followed him toward the waiting black sedan.

"So you're really not going to tell me?" Karma inquired as the sedan snaked its way through the busy New York City streets.

CJ shook his head.

"Okay."

Karma watched the traffic for a while and then looked down at the four inches of leather seat between them. "Why don't you come a little closer?" she suggested, patting the seat.

CJ smiled and inched over until their hips touched. He placed his hand on her knee.

"Fresh," Karma exclaimed, shoving his hand off.

He quickly placed it back, this time allowing his middle finger to make tiny circles on her flesh. Karma felt a slight thrill streak through her body.

She placed her hand over his and guided it up her thigh, bringing it to halt at the hem of her skirt.

"Tease." Claude laughed, and bent over and kissed her.

"You taste good," he said, his lips inches from her face. She could feel his hot breath on her lips.

"So do you."

They kissed again with a bit more urgency. CJ's hand slipped beneath her skirt, up her thigh, and settled between her legs. He pulled air between his teeth and jerked his head back in surprise.

She didn't have any underwear on.

Karma grinned wickedly.

Claude smiled back, leaned in, and began kissing her again as his fingers explored her damp den.

He rubbed his thumb rhythmically against her clitoris, and Karma's back arched in gleeful response.

"Oh, oh, CJ," she moaned as she spread her legs wider. He inserted his finger and began to move it in a come-hither motion.

Karma's head rolled against the leather headrest.

"Ah-oh-ah-ah-ah," she whimpered as she scaled Climax Mountain. "I-I-I . . ."

Claude pressed his mouth against hers, muffling her orgasmic screams.

The sedan came to a halt and Karma, pulling her skirt down, brushed her hair from her face and saw that they'd arrived at a heliport. Her eyes popped with surprise.

"Just where are you taking me, Mr. CJ?"

"New Hampshire," Claude responded as he retrieved a handkerchief from his pocket and wiped Karma's juices from his fingers.

"New Hampshire! In that!" Karma squealed, pointing at the helicopter.

"Ever been in one?"

She shook her head no. And she wasn't sure she wanted to be in one now. Planes were fine, but a helicopter?

"Come on," he said, grabbing her by the hand and pulling her from the car. "You'll love it."

CJ strapped her in and then himself. The noise from the whirling propellers was deafening until he fitted the headset over her ears. "Can you hear me?" he asked, speaking into the mouthpiece of the headset.

Karma nodded her head.

"Don't be nervous, it's perfectly safe. I've done this a million times."

He tapped the pilot on the shoulder and twirled his index finger.

Up they went.

For the first fifteen minutes of the flight, Karma's eyes were squeezed tightly shut. One hand gripped the side of her seat and the other held fast to CJ's hand.

She could hear him offering words of comfort through her headphones, but it did little good. Her heart was racing a mile a minute.

Twenty minutes in she was able to convince herself to open first one eye and then the next. The view below was staggeringly beautiful. "How long will it take?"

"Just another hour or so."

They set down in a clearing of dense forest about one hundred feet from a log-cabin-style mansion.

"CJ?"

"Yes," CJ responded, removing his headset and turning to look at her.

"Who are you?"

It was an honest question. One that needed to be asked. She didn't know this man from squat and no one knew that she was with him or that she was even in New Hampshire. If that's where they really were.

He could realistically slit her throat, feed her into a wood chipper and sprinkle her remains in the forest, and get away with it.

"Why," CJ gave her an earnest look, "I'm the man of your dreams."

A short balding gentleman with the bluest eyes Karma had ever seen greeted them at the door.

"Welcome back, sir. And welcome to you, madam."

Karma straightened her back. She hadn't been referred to as madam since she left Europe.

The house had to be six thousand square feet and sure did look like it cost a good chunk of change.

"Do you own this?" Karma asked in open amazement.

"Yes."

She followed CJ and the butler through the foyer, if you could call it that. It was more like the expansive lobby of a five-star hotel.

Each room she passed seemed grander than the last. And although Karma was no art collector, she knew the great ones when she saw them. And CJ had a number of Rembrandts and Degas.

The butler showed them out onto a sweeping veranda that offered unparalleled views of a sparkling blue lake and the woods beyond.

There they enjoyed an intimate lunch, served by the small butler, who had donned white gloves for the occasion.

"Are you impressed?" CJ's eyes twinkled knowingly.

She was, very much so, and nodded her head yes.

She supposed he would be expecting sex. She didn't mind. He deserved it. Especially after his performance in the car. She could imagine what he'd be like in the bed.

But she was concerned. He had been nothing but a gentleman the entire time and she wondered if CJ had a Jekyll and Hyde personality.

"When's your birthday?" she asked suddenly.

CJ set his water glass down and smiled at her. "Why?"

"Are you a Gemini?"

"Again," he said, leaning back into his chair, "why?"

Karma continued to ignore his question. "I think you might be a Gemini, because this man sitting across from me is similar to the man I had brunch with two weeks ago, but nothing like the man on the telephone earlier this week or the naughty finger-fucker in the car. Hence my vote for Gemini."

CJ laughed heartily before using the linen napkin to dab the corners of his mouth. "Oh, that," he said, and Karma was sure she saw him blush. "That was just a little wicked foreplay. I thought women liked foreplay? Maybe I was wrong."

With that he gave her a penetrating look. One that left her feeling stripped bare. She felt herself falter, as if she'd stumbled on the catwalk.

Dropping her eyes, she said, "No, you weren't wrong."

CJ grinned smugly and lifted his water glass to his lips. He could see right through her. He knew that she had not always been the beauty she was now. She didn't wear it the way the ones who'd owned their beauty from adolescence wore theirs—like an old familiar coat.

Karma's coat hung a little slack.

She was like a little girl playing grown-up.

He and his dick would show her what *real* grown-up was like.

"Listen," he said, looking down at his watch. "I do have an important business meeting to attend before we head back to New York."

Karma just looked at him. Surely he wasn't going to leave her there?

"I'm going to be gone for an hour or so. You'll be perfectly fine with Winston. And if you want you can take a swim," he said, nodding his head toward the lake. He was already out of his chair.

"Watch a movie in the media room, play any number of games in the game room, or just take a long walk."

Karma was speechless as he sauntered over and kissed her gently on the forehead.

"Okay?" he said, looming over her, hands stuck deep into the pockets of his slacks, his face a mask of seriousness.

"Okay," Karma heard herself say.

# 23

The trees whisked by at nearly seventy miles per hour. Claude liked speed; he liked power; it got him excited, got him hard.

He rubbed at the ever-growing stiffness between his legs and a sharp thrill climbed his spine.

He chuckled to himself as he threw the car into fourth gear. The candy-apple-red Porsche leaped forward like a wild animal. CJ tightened his grip on the wheel.

A Kanye West tune banged out of the surround-sound speakers, and CJ bounced his head to the beat.

He pushed the gear stick up, shifting the car into fifth gear; the speedometer climbed to ninety-five.

He was on top of the fucking world!

. . .

The New York Times bestselling book *The Secret* had recently had a ripple effect on the world's population, and they'd all had a collective "Aha" moment.

But Claude had been a participant in the power-of-attraction game for a very long time now. Which is how he'd accumulated so much wealth in so little time. He was just a couple of million dollars away from being a billionaire.

Money attracted more money.

There would never be a lack of pussy, no matter that Jill Scott threatened it in one of her songs—you born and find pussy, you gonna die and leave it here—his mother always said.

Claude had decided that he wanted the sex, but also he wanted love and commitment. Which is why he began collecting wives.

Black men talked about how back in the days of ancient Africa, men were allowed to, expected to, have multiple wives, and that was their inherent right, even now in the twenty-first century.

They talked that shit, ignorant of the fact that all of the wives were to be treated equally, and that ran the gamut—housing, finance, love, and sex.

These knuckleheaded brothers nowadays just wanted unlimited access to a variety of pussy and none of the responsibility that went along with it.

And so CJ and his brothers in clandestine polygamy had found a way to have their cake and eat it too!

With his lifestyle there was hardly ever a bad family day. All of his wives were housed in fabulous homes with a nice allowance and late-model car.

His children, of which he currently had six, with one on the way, were all in private school.

They were his future and he had to admit that he felt like God whenever a new little Justine came squealing into the world.

CJ was a man, like many other men, and he knew very early on that no one woman would be able to satisfy him on any level, and so the decision had been made to acquire a number of women who, put together, composed the perfect one. So far, it was working out just swell.

His wives were always happy to see him and he made sure he planned his visits around their menstrual cycles so he could always look forward to passionate welcome-home sex.

But he was still a man, and while he did philander, it wasn't at the rate he would have if not for his many wives.

*Claude rehearsed his story* again and again until it rang true even to himself. Nadia was smart; she listened well and had almost tripped him up a few times. But that was before she had the twins, Jackson and James, and got the pug called Danish. Now she had her all-American dream, husband and lavish home included.

Claude suddenly snapped his fingers, shifting the gears from fifth to fourth and down to third; he felt safe enough to take one hand off the steering wheel and reach into his attaché case.

Pulling out a diamond-encrusted wedding ring, he slipped it on just as he guided the Porsche into the driveway.

Nadia was standing out front, her hands on her slim hips as she scrutinized the dwarf roses around the edge of the house.

Nadia was the product of a Senegalese mother and a Scottish father. She was the most exotic woman CJ had ever seen.

She spun around at the sound of the wheels crunching over the gravel and then her face brightened and the smile that first stole his heart appeared.

"Hey, baby," she greeted him, throwing her arms around his neck and hugging him.

He hugged her back, taking the opportunity to cup her small round bottom in his hands.

"Look who's home, boys," Nadia sang as Claude followed her into the family room, where the twins were sitting opposite each other, eyes locked and motionless.

CJ stopped in mid-stride. "Something new?" he turned and asked Nadia.

"Yeah, about a week now."

Claude shook his head. His twins were a little freaky. But every doctor he'd taken them to said that they were normal, healthy two-and-a-half-year-olds.

"Hey, guys!" Claude exclaimed as he came and stood over them.

The twins did not acknowledge his presence.

"I think they do things like this just to upset you, Claude."

"What?"

"Well, you're never here. I think they resent not having their father around."

"Oh, that's just silly, Nadia."

"Is it? I know I resent not having my husband around." Nadia's tone was wounded.

"I thought we were beyond this, Nadia?"

"I guess we're not."

Claude walked to her and wrapped his arms around her. "I told you when we got married that my plan was to be a billionaire by the time I was fifty. After that, you and the boys will have me all to yourselves all of the time. But in order for me to make that billion-dollar mark I have to work, and unfortunately my work keeps me on the road and away from the people I love the most."

Nadia nodded her head. "I know I'm being silly, but can I help that I miss you?"

"I miss you too, baby." Claude bent and kissed her neck. "That's why I flew in from Arizona just to spend a few hours with you and the boys," he added, and slipped his hand beneath her T-shirt.

Nadia's whole body began to quake. It had been nearly a month since they'd last had sex.

"We're still going to take the boys to Disney World next month, right?" she whispered as Claude unhooked her bra.

"Yes, everything is booked. We leave on the sixteenth."

"Lori!" Nadia yelled for the nanny as she grabbed Claude's hand and started toward their bedroom.

"Yes, ma'am?"

"Watch the boys while me and my husband get reacquainted."

She'd sulked all the way back to New York, even though CJ had apologized profusely and tried everything to get her to crack a smile.

How could he have done her that way? Leaving her in a strange house with not one but two strange men—the butler and the helicopter pilot!

And CJ hadn't returned until midnight. Midnight!

"This is my life, Karma. If you want to be a part of it, you have to know that sometimes things like this are going to happen."

That was his lame explanation.

When he dropped her off at her apartment it was nearly three in the morning. The car had barely come to a stop before Karma flung the door open. She had one foot on the ground when CJ caught her by the wrist. "You're being childish, Karma."

Karma just glared at him.

"If you don't want me to call you again, just say so."

She hadn't said a word, just turned and stormed into the building.

Why hadn't she said, "Don't ever call me again, you stupid fucking dick!"

Why hadn't she said that?

Karma turned roughly over in her bed. It was nearly seven in the morning and she'd not slept one wink. The question haunted her and every time she closed her eyes it glowed bright in the darkness of her mind.

# 24

Crystal rolled over and was surprised to find Claude standing over her.

"Hey, baby." She sighed and reached out for him. "I wasn't expecting you back until tomorrow."

"It is tomorrow," Claude said as he climbed into bed beside her.

Crystal looked over at the digital clock. It was just after four in the morning.

Taking her into his arms, he held her close against his chest and kissed the top of her head. "Do you know how much I love you?"

Crystal felt she did and so responded, "Yes."

"No, I don't think you do," Claude said, and his chest heaved with emotion. "I can't wait to make you my wife, Crystal Atkins."

"And I can't wait to be your wife, Claude Justine."

. . .

The following morning Crystal flipped first one pancake and then the next. She felt so blessed to be alive and in love.

"Smells great," Claude said as he walked into the kitchen and placed a kiss on Javid's forehead and then Kayla's.

"Morning, Daddy," Kayla chimed.

"Morning, Daddy," Javid followed. He had begun calling Claude Daddy. At first Crystal objected, but Claude said it was only natural. He would feel left out if she forbade it.

"I guess you're right," Crystal had finally acquiesced. And anyway, Javid seemed *clear* on who his real daddy was; he and Neville spoke on the phone at least twice a week.

"Aren't you going to have any pancakes, Mommy?" Javid asked when Crystal joined her family at the breakfast table with just a cup of tea and grapefruit.

"Yes, Mommy, aren't you?" Claude mocked in a high-pitched tone.

Crystal waved her hand at him and then turned to Javid and said, "Mommy is getting a little wide in the hips, baby. So she has to lay off the pancakes for a while."

Javid seemed satisfied with the response and turned his attention back to his food.

"I like your hips," Claude said as he reached over and grabbed hold of her right hip.

Crystal blushed and gave him a look that said, "Not in front of the children."

"So what do you have planned for today?" Claude asked as he helped Crystal clear the table and load the dishwasher.

He was actually going to be home for the entire day.

"Well, Shelly invited me over for lunch at her place."

Claude turned around abruptly. The move was so sudden that the plate slipped from his hand and went crashing to the floor.

"Oh damn," he said as he walked over to the utility closet to retrieve the broom and dustpan. "You know I don't like that woman." His voice was quivering, and Crystal couldn't remember a time she'd ever seen Claude come undone. He actually seemed on the verge of anger.

"Yeah, but I do," Crystal said as she took the dustpan from his hand.

"I forbid you to go!" Claude barked, snatching the dustpan from her and flinging it across the room.

Crystal jumped at the ferocity in his voice.

Forbid?

"Lower your voice, Claude, you're scaring the children."

"I don't give a damn. This is my house and I'll raise my voice if I want to!"

For a brief moment he resembled a small child experiencing a temper tantrum, balled fists, red-faced and all.

Crystal had never seen this side of him. In her mind that other shoe that had been dangling in the air above her head over the past few months came crashing down to the floor.

Kayla took Javid by the hand and led him away from the commotion.

"Claude, you're being irrational—"

"Irrational? You haven't seen irrational," and with that Claude began snatching open the kitchen cabinets, grabbing plate after plate, flinging them to the floor.

"Claude!"

When it was all over, every dish they owned lay in pieces at their feet.

And just as suddenly as the storm arrived, it slipped away.

Crystal was cowering in the corner, frozen with fear, not sure if he would turn his anger on her.

The house was silent as Claude stared down at the mess he'd made. When his eyes found Crystal, she saw that his face had reverted back to that of the man she knew and loved.

Claude shook his head as if coming out of a fog, and then a look of surprise streaked across his face. "Oh my God, Crystal," he said, coming toward her, his arms outstretched. Crystal shrank away, trying to press herself further into the corner.

Claude backed off. "I'm sorry, baby. I'm so sorry, sometimes I just get—"

Crystal slid along the wall. Claude saw the horror and fear swimming in her eyes.

"Baby, Crystal . . . I would never hurt you, please don't—" He suddenly broke down in tears and crumpled to his knees. "I didn't mean to, sometimes I just get so angry . . ." he trailed off, sobbing.

Crystal watched him for a moment. Part of her screamed: Get your child, get his child and run!

But the other part said: Go to him.

She went to him, gathered him into her arms and rocked him until his tears stopped.

They clung to each other as he murmured "I'm sorry" and "I love you" over and over in her ear.

# 25

Karma didn't really want to go.

"Aw, come on!" Geneva screeched over the phone line. "You said you would!"

Karma rolled her eyes. Yes, she had said she would go, but she'd agreed to that a week ago and so much had happened since then. Well, not really that much, but what had happened was still weighing down on her.

She hadn't heard from CJ since what she'd come to refer to as "the New Hampshire incident." Well, that wasn't exactly true— he had sent her two dozen white roses and a few e-mails from Bangkok, where he claimed to be on business.

Really and truly she just wanted to sit at home and sulk.

"I don't know, Geneva, all the way out to New Jersey, and on the bus?"

. . .

Crystal picked them up from the bus stop. Geneva and Crystal had known each other for so long that there wasn't much Crystal could hide from her, or vice versa.

"What the hell is wrong with you?" Geneva said as soon as she looked into Crystal's face.

Ignoring her, Crystal climbed out of the car, brushed passed Geneva and walked straight to Karma.

"Hello, I'm Crystal Atkins, so nice to finally meet you. Geneva has said nothing but good things about you."

"Yeah, yeah," Geneva said, stepping between the two women and pushing her hands into her hips. "You don't look right. That man working your nerves?"

"Just a bumpy start to the day," Crystal said as she climbed back into the car. "I'll be fine once I get some wine in me."

They drove along in silence for a while as Geneva gazed out the window like an eager puppy. "It's nice out here in the country," she commented.

Both Crystal and Karma laughed at Geneva's observation.

"I wouldn't quite call this country," Crystal corrected her. "The suburbs, yes, but not the country."

"It is nice though," Karma offered from the backseat. "I want to live like this one day."

They turned into the driveway and Geneva let off a long whistle. "Your house is beautiful."

Crystal started to say: Well, it's not my house, as I was so dutifully informed this morning.

Geneva climbed out of the car, her eyes wide as saucers. "I can't wait to meet Claude."

"Maybe later on, he took the kids to the Bronx Zoo today. He should be back before you guys head home."

Crystal gave them a tour of the house and found herself cringing behind every "oooh" and "aaah" that emanated from the ladies.

"Karma, didn't I tell you that my girl had hit the jackpot!" Geneva beamed.

Karma nodded in agreement even though her insides were knotted with envy.

"So where does Shelly live?" Geneva asked, her voice climbing with excitement.

"Just across the street."

Geneva rushed to the front door and yanked it open. "Which one is it?"

"It's the bi-level brick with the green shutters."

"That's it?" Geneva sounded disappointed. "I thought it would be a bit . . ."

"Bigger?" Karma was behind her, peering over her shoulder.

"Yeah, and I dunno, more luxurious."

Crystal pulled the door closed. "She told you she leads a simple life."

"Welcome," Shelly offered with a bright smile. "Come in, come in."

"This is for you." Crystal handed her a bottle of wine wrapped in a white fur cozy.

"That's so nice, you really shouldn't have," Shelly said, and then pulled the bottle out. "Girl, you been spying on me?"

"Me? No!" Crystal yelped in surprise.

"Oh, 'cause Sauvignon Blanc is my all-time favorite wine."

"Oh." Crystal relaxed again.

"Hey, Geneva, so glad you could make it." Shelly gave her a tight hug. "And you brought a friend?"

"Yes, this is Karma Jackson. Karma, this is the *famous* Shenelody Miller," Geneva proudly announced.

Karma smiled and offered her hand, but Shelly pushed it away before throwing her arms around her.

"We hug in this house, girl."

"My house is very small," Shelly explained as they moved toward the rear of the house, "just three bedrooms and my study downstairs."

Geneva was deflated. It didn't seem as if Shelly was going to give them a tour.

Shelly slid the sliding glass door open. "I have everything set up outside."

"Aw, man, why didn't you tell me she had a pool, Crystal, I could have brought my swimsuit," Geneva moaned as she walked over to the edge of the oval-shaped pool.

Crystal lowered herself down onto one of the four cushioned chaise longues. "I didn't know."

Karma sat down alongside Crystal and kicked off her sandals. "I could really get used to this," she proclaimed as she took the glass of wine Shelly offered her.

Geneva bounded over. "Me too, girl. Maybe I should write a book. Shoot, maybe we all should write a book."

Shelly sat down in one of the swivel patio chairs, crossed her legs, and looked out over the backyard. "I can't complain. I've been very blessed."

Karma pulled her shades out of her pocketbook and placed them on her face. Some people are more blessed than others, she thought to herself.

. . .

Crystal and Claude arrived at the driveway entrance at the same time.

"Hey, you." Claude rolled down the window and called to Crystal, who offered him a smile before turning into the driveway.

Inside the garage, Claude climbed out of the new Jag he'd purchased a week earlier and rested his arms on the top of the car.

"What?" Crystal asked when she stepped out. "Why are you looking at me like that?"

"Because you're so beautiful and because I love you."

Crystal blushed. She had tried all day long to stay mad at him, but with each glass of wine and with every "that man done did me wrong" story that passed between her, Shelly, Karma and Geneva, Crystal slowly came to realize that she had a good man, a damn good man, and so the anger just disappeared.

"I love you too, baby."

The children were passed out in the backseat. Crystal lifted Javid from his car seat and Claude hoisted Kayla up and into his arms.

After undressing the children and tucking them into bed, Claude and Crystal met up in the master bedroom. He pulled her to him and kissed her. "You taste like a winery," he joked before kissing her again.

After their lovemaking, they curled into each other, Crystal's head pressed against his chest; she was slowly being lulled to sleep by the rhythm of his heartbeat. "What time is your flight in the morning?"

Claude yawned. "I'm on the nine o'clock."

"And back when?"

Claude thought about it for a moment. "Um, Wednesday."

He gently stroked her hair and whispered, "I didn't even ask how you girls enjoyed yourselves over at Shelly's."

He knew that if Shelly had insinuated anything about their past together Crystal would have already confronted him about it. Apparently, Shelly was adhering to the terms of their agreement.

"Oh," Crystal yawned, "we had a nice time. You know, just girl talk."

"Did you talk about me?"

"Mr. Conceited," Crystal teased, "bulletin, the world doesn't revolve around you, you know." She laughed.

Of course it did, Claude mused.

"No, but seriously, Shelly is really very nice and so humble for what she's accomplished."

Thanks to me, Claude thought.

"The four of us really had a nice time."

"Four?"

"Yeah, Geneva ended up bringing a friend of hers along. She's a really pretty girl, with the oddest name. Her name is—"

"Moooooooommmmmmmmmy!" Javid shrieked from his bedroom. "I peeeeeed the bed!"

Crystal looked at Claude and sighed. "Motherhood," she muttered as she climbed from the bed.

"No," Claude said, tossing the comforter from his body. "Parenthood," he said, resting one hand on her waist and following her out of the room.

# 26

Jaihara rubbed her swollen belly and the baby shifted beneath her hand. She grinned. The movement never ceased to amaze her.

"Okay, Mrs. Justine, this is going to be a little cold," the doctor said before she squeezed the jelly onto her stomach.

This was her fourth sonogram.

Each time the doctor assured her that the child she was carrying, her first, was healthy. But she wasn't taking any chances; she'd miscarried once and so she wanted to be extra careful with this one. And so demanded that she have a sonogram every month until she delivered.

It wasn't like her medical insurance was footing the bill for it (like they would!). Her husband was a wealthy man; five hundred dollars to Claude was like five dollars to a regular Joe.

Jaihara gripped Claude's hand. "It's still a boy," she teased.

Claude grinned and nodded as he stole a glance at the clock on the wall. He had a three o'clock flight back to New York.

"And he's still healthy," the doctor added.

"Promise me you'll be here for the birth of our son, Claude," Jaihara pressed as they walked toward the Range Rover. "It's the—"

"I know, baby, I know, the fourth of July."

"Yeah," Jaihara beamed. "Independence Day."

Claude opened the door of the vehicle and helped her in.

"So are we good with Joshua as a name?" she asked as she flipped open the glove compartment and rummaged through it until she located the lip balm.

"I thought we had settled on Jordan?"

Claude smiled inside. Jaihara could never make up her mind. There had been only one decision she didn't need to toss around and that was on the day he'd asked her to marry him. Everything after that had been a long, drawn-out ordeal; the house, the color of the walls, the furniture, the type of car, and she'd already had the nursery repainted six times, and now the baby's name had changed. Although she had remained committed to a name that started with J.

Just twenty-two years old, Jaihara was the youngest of his wives. Hawaiian by birth and lineage, she had long wavy hair and eyes the color of onyx.

He loved her innocence, loved it so much that he'd claimed it for himself a year ago on a secluded beach in Maui.

Jaihara, so young, so inexperienced, so eager to learn! The sex between them was always amazing. She did whatever he requested. He was her world and she wanted to do whatever pleased him.

Claude sighed as he navigated the Range Rover down Ventura Boulevard and toward home.

The phone on his hip began to vibrate. "Ugh," Jaihara cried, "can't I have you all to myself for five minutes?"

Claude patted her knee assuredly. "Don't be like that," he said before plucking the phone from his waist and peering at the number.

It was Karma. He'd let the call go to voice mail.

"See, baby," he said as he levied a little more pressure on the gas pedal, "that was a very important call from Hong Kong, but you mean more to me than the two million dollars I just lost by not taking the call. Now if that ain't love I don't know what is!"

*Jaihara waddled into the bedroom,* naked as the day she was born. Her belly was round and beautiful and her breasts had swelled to a remarkable size. As she moved closer, her nipples seemed to reach out to him.

"Am I still sexy to you, Claude?" Jaihara questioned in her best little-girl voice.

"Of course," he said, grabbing her by her waist and pulling her gently to him.

He kissed her belly first and then raised his head and began sucking hungrily on her jutting nipples.

Jaihara pressed her hands against the back of his head, urging him to suck harder. He obliged, and Jaihara groaned as she tossed her head back and settled herself down onto his lap.

She was already dripping wet when she began to slowly grind herself against his knee.

"Aiy, aiy," she growled as she stepped up her pace. "It feels so good, Daddy, it feels so good!"

Claude loved it when she called him Daddy and began to suck more eagerly.

Jaihara dug her fingers into his skull; she was riding his knee as if it were a prize stallion. Her body twitched each time she managed to hit what she referred to as her "goody-spot." And when she hit it Claude knew, not just from the twitching and jerking her body fell into, but from Jaihara's breathless chant that always followed: "Goodie-goodie-goodie-goodie . . ."

Jaihara's body jerked one last time and then she went stiff, except for her legs, which shook as if a bolt of electricity was ripping through them.

"Aaaaaah," she cried out into the darkness of their bedroom before she dropped her head onto his shoulder and began to weep.

"Oh Claude," she whimpered as the tears rolled down his back.

She always cried afterward. Their lovemaking was always very emotional for her.

Claude pulled her tight against him and stroked her back.

Glancing over at the digital alarm clock on the nightstand, he knew he wouldn't be making his three o'clock plane back to New York; it was already after one and there was no way he could just up and leave Jaihara in the state she was in.

She was the most fragile of his wives. He would have to spend a few hours comforting her and reassuring her that he loved her and the baby growing inside of her.

He would have to call the airline and reschedule for the seven o'clock.

# 27

Karma looked at the package again. It had her name and company address typed neatly on the label, but there was no return address.

The package had arrived just before she'd left the office and now it sat on her kitchen table as she and Seneca stood staring at it.

"Well, open it," Seneca urged for the third time. "You're acting like a freak."

"Don't call me that."

"I didn't call you a freak, I said you're *acting* like one."

Seneca was right. She was behaving like a freak, but something about the package got her skin to crawling; she'd almost tossed it in the trash on the subway platform, that's how intense the feeling was.

"Maybe it's from that guy you won't tell me anything about."

Karma looked over at Seneca, who was now sprawled out on

the couch, her index finger stuck deep into her ear foraging for wax. Suddenly Karma couldn't figure why it was she kept her as a friend. Mentally she shifted Seneca over to the acquaintance column of her life.

Finally Karma took a deep breath and ripped open the package, and as she did she could hear Seneca scurry from the couch and to her side.

"Wow," Seneca exclaimed as she stared down at the ivory-colored silk teddy. "That looks expensive," she said, reaching her stubby fingers out to touch the material.

Karma snatched it quickly away. "You just had your finger in your ear."

Seneca rolled her eyes and stood back on one leg.

There was an envelope lying on the red tissue paper the teddy had been wrapped in. Seneca swooped it up, opened it, and read the note aloud: "Karma, meet me at the Pierre Hotel this Tuesday at eight p.m. Give me a chance to make it all up to you. Wear this with stilettos and nothing else. I will send a car to meet you at work. CJ"

Seneca's eyes popped. "What the hell?"

Karma just smirked at her before snatching the note from her hand.

"Now that," Seneca said, "is some freaky shit!"

"Shut up," Karma said as she walked off toward her bedroom.

"Is this what you guys do?" Seneca asked, following close behind. "I mean, I like it. Okay, I love that kind of shit!"

Karma tossed the teddy onto the bed. Who did this CJ think he was? No phone call in two weeks, just a few three-word e-mails, and now this? What did he think she was, some kind of call girl? He never asked, just demanded and assumed she would do whatever he wanted her to do.

And so far she had, hadn't she?

She was so stupid!

"I really need to be alone right now," Karma spouted suddenly.

Seneca was wounded. "What? Why?"

"I just do."

"Why are you mad at me? I didn't send you the teddy."

"Seneca, please." Karma's voice was stern.

"Whatever," Seneca said as she turned and walked out of the bedroom. "You may be Karma Jackson, but you still got a lot of Mildred Johnson's ways."

"What?"

"You've got to loosen up. The man wants to play sex games, so what? Stop being so conservative and let your wild side out of its cage sometimes."

Seneca was at the front door, her hand on the knob. "Every man you meet is not a potential mate. Sometimes they're just for fuck's sake."

She swung the door open and walked out.

Karma stood and watched as the door slowly swung closed.

Everything Seneca had said was true. But Karma was no prude, she didn't have a problem with casual sex, it's just that she wanted to be more than a toy to this man.

He was Grade A, something special, husband material, and she wanted nothing more than to be a wife.

# 28

"Hey, baby." Claude's sexy voice slithered through the telephone lines, wrapping itself all around her.

Crystal pressed her thighs together; just the sound of his voice made her moist.

"Hey, yourself."

Claude said he was still in LA. He had to extend his trip another few days, but assured her that he would be back on Friday.

"Miss me?"

"All day and all night." Crystal giggled as she flipped over onto her back with a little grunt.

"Are you in bed?"

She was ashamed to say that she was in bed in the middle of the afternoon. But she'd had a restless night and decided when she put the kids down for their nap that she would do the same for herself.

"Yes, I am. But you see——" She started to explain herself but Claude cut her off.

"Really? That's nice," he purred. "Are you naked?"

Of course she wasn't naked. But she would play along.

"Uh-huh," she giggled as she slipped her hand down between her legs.

Claude hadn't allowed himself to cum. He would save that for Karma.

Women weren't the only ones who could fake it, he snickered to himself as he climbed into the marble shower stall of his bathroom en suite at the Pierre Hotel.

Jaihara had needed more comforting than expected, and so Claude ended up taking the red-eye from LAX, which got him into New York around seven in the morning.

"I love my life!" he bellowed as the hot water came rushing out of the faucet and crashing onto his skin.

It was nearly ten o'clock; he suspected that if he'd read Karma right (he had a knack for reading women), the front desk would be calling up soon to announce her arrival.

Claude's plan was to meet her at the door, buck-naked. If she ran, it was no sweat off his back. If she stayed, he'd treat her to the best fuck of her life.

He flexed his muscles as he stood and admired himself in the vanity mirror. What had he done to be so goddamn good-looking? Not just good-looking, but smart, successful, powerful and rich? He had it all, didn't he?

And his story wasn't some movie-of-the-week tearjerker either. His father wasn't an abusive alcoholic who couldn't keep a job and his mother wasn't some strung-out addict who'd met a tragic end at the mouth of a dark alley.

His father, Adam, was a successful dentist, and his mother, Vivian, a homemaker with a master's degree in art.

Claude grew up in Freeport, Long Island, went to public school, excelled in sports, didn't make prom king but got to fuck the prom queen, and then went off to Pennsylvania State University on a full scholarship.

The only time Claude ever worked for someone other than himself was when he was sixteen years old and spent the summer as a lifeguard.

In college, he'd kept mostly to himself. He liked to read the *Wall Street Journal* and daydream about his bright future.

He convinced his father to buy some stock in AOL. Claude had explained to his father that the Internet was going to be what the telephone had been a century earlier. "And you remember what happened to that Ma Bell stock, don't you?"

In a few years AOL made them all rich. The rest, as they say, is history.

That had been the first of a number of wise choices.

The blaring sound of the phone cut through his musing. "Hello?"

"Miss Karma Jackson is here, sir. Shall I send her up?"

CJ looked over at the clock. She was eight minutes early.

"Yes, please do."

# 29

Shelly stared at the blinking cursor on her computer screen. It had been blinking that way for nearly twenty minutes straight.

"Starting is the hardest part," she whispered to herself.

She went through this each and every time she sat down to write a new book. It made her crazy.

Glancing over at the desk calendar, her eyes fell on the number fifty, written in red marker beneath the date, July 10.

Shelly was supposed to have fifty pages and she didn't even have a first sentence.

Jumping up from her desk, she strolled over to the window and lit a cigarette. Inhaling deeply, she stared out onto the street, which was empty except for the mailman.

She had ideas swirling around in her head like a windstorm, but couldn't seem to settle on just one.

"Just write!" her mind screamed at her. "It's not like this is something new. It always comes together in the end!"

It was true, she thought as she stubbed the cigarette out and walked back over to her desk. It did always come together in the end.

*His hands kneaded her thighs, slowly turning her muscles to butter. His hands were like fire on Magda's skin and she fought to contain herself.*

*Am I pressing too hard? Aldo, her masseuse, inquired.*

*No, Magda responded, and then a groan escaped her and she threw caution to the wind, tossing the towel to the floor and exposing her nakedness.*

*Miss Magda! Aldo cried in surprise.*

*Magda turned over and spread her legs; she wanted Aldo to see her Eden, already dripping with her nectar.*

*I want you to drink from my vessel, Aldo, Magda cried as she clutched his wrist and tugged him downward.*

*Aldo's lips brushed her thigh and then she felt his tongue . . .*

Shelly suddenly pushed back from her desk. "Damn," she muttered as her wheeled chair rolled to the wall and stopped with a bump.

She hated writing sex scenes; they made her hot.

"Whatever," she said aloud, and rolled back to the desk, where she opened the bottom drawer and pulled out a black and gold vibrator.

Slipping out of her shorts and thong, she propped her legs up on the desk and leaned back in the chair, forcing it to tilt dangerously back on its stem.

Shelly flicked the switch and the vibrator came trembling to life.

Teasing her clitoris with the pointed tip of the device, her eyes picked over the various framed newspaper articles and pictures of herself with friends and family members, until finally her eyes fell on the framed movie poster of *Training Day*, which pictured Denzel as the bad boy cop of her dreams.

She steadied her gaze and slid the vibrator deep inside her. "Oooh," she moaned, "Denzel, Denzel," as her body bucked in the leather chair, sending her wetness slipping down the crack of her behind, where it puddled beneath her cheeks.

Shelly moved the vibrator in and out at such a rapid rate that her orgasm jumped the starter bell and caught her off guard.

A scream exploded in her throat as pleasure ripped through her abdomen.

She wanted to smoke a cigarette, but was too weak to move. She imagined she must have looked a pitiful sight, her shorts and underwear strewn on the floor, her feet resting on the edge of the desk, knees splayed wide, exposing the creamy-colored goo of her orgasm.

*"Crystal?"*

Shelly was truly surprised.

Crystal smiled, a bit embarrassed. "Hi," she said, giving her a little two-finger wave. "I hope I didn't interrupt you?"

She had interrupted her. Shelly had masturbated two more times, finally releasing enough tension to pound out twenty very good pages. When Crystal rang the bell, she had just hit her stride.

"No, not at all," Shelly lied as she smiled down at Javid and Kayla. "Come in."

"I was going stir crazy and just wanted a little adult company."

"Well, come in," Shelly said again.

"No, no, I actually wanted to know if you wanted to join me . . . I mean us, for a walk?"

Shelly considered Crystal for a minute and then thought about her work in progress; she could hear it calling to her from the study, but Crystal looked so needy.

"Okay, no problem, let me just grab my keys."

Shelly couldn't remember the last time she'd been to the playground. She and Crystal were quiet for a while as they watched Kayla and Javid rip and run with the other children.

"Gosh," Shelly said with a sigh, "remember when you had that type of energy?"

Crystal nodded her head and took a tiny sip from her water bottle. "It seems so long ago."

"I keep telling myself I'm going to start running, bike riding, something, anything to get this old body in shape!"

"Old? Please," Crystal quipped with a roll of her eyes. "You look great!"

"You flatter me, Crystal."

Crystal turned and looked Shelly square in the eye. "We've got to be the same age."

"Really? How old are you, thirty-three?"

Crystal beamed. "Now you're flattering me. I'm forty!"

"You look damn good, girl."

"Thanks. So what are you? Forty-one?"

Shelly gave her a sly smile. "Fifty-one."

Crystal's mouth dropped open. "You are a goddamn liar!" she screamed, and leveled a slap on Shelly's knee.

"Ow! Am not." Shelly laughed as she retrieved her wallet from the denim Coach swing pack she carried.

"See?"

Crystal stared at Shelly's license picture and the birth date beneath it. It was true.

"Shelly, you look fabulous!"

"Well, you know what they say," Shelly said as she flipped the wallet closed. "Fifty is the new forty!"

Their conversation jumped from books to music to favorite foods, and all the while Crystal marveled at Shelly's tight, flawless skin, straight white teeth, and washboard stomach.

"Stop staring, Crystal, you're freaking me out," Shelly complained.

"I'm sorry, girl, I just can't believe it. When I grow up I want to be just like you. Or at least have your body!"

Shelly blushed, looked at her watch and announced she had to get back home.

"I understand, girl," Crystal said. "I appreciate the company."

"Hey," Shelly said as she rose from the bench and stuck a Newport between her lips, "let's get together and do a spa day or something?"

Crystal's face lit up. "I would love that!"

"Invite your girls, Geneva and . . ." Shelly snapped her fingers.

"Karma," Crystal reminded her.

"Yes, Karma."

Shelly exhaled before leaning over and whispering in a conspiratorial tone, "There is something about that chick, I think she's got a story."

Crystal laughed. "Don't we all? Hey, maybe I should start writing a novel?"

"Maybe you should," Shelly threw over her shoulder as she strolled away.

Crystal wasn't sure, but she thought she heard Shelly add, "If you discover what I know about your man, you'll have a number-one bestseller on your hands."

# 30

Shelly poured herself a drink, a tall vodka and grapefruit juice, and carried it out to the patio.

She eased herself down onto the chaise longue and sipped. That wasn't a nice thing to have said, she scolded herself.

And even though she'd barely said it above a whisper, she knew she'd still been close enough for Crystal to have overheard.

Shelly regretted it now, but at that moment she wanted Crystal to know with whom she was lying down every fourth night or so.

Claude Justine, the new millennium Valentino!

"Ha." A bitter laugh escaped Shelly's throat.

She took another sip of the drink to wash away the nasty taste his name left in her mouth.

Claude Justine, a man who had many wives and concubines. A polygamist to the twentieth power!

She drained the glass then.

LOVER MAN  ·  143

Shelly had fallen under his spell exactly eighteen years ago. She'd become his wife and given birth to his daughter, *their* daughter, and then she found out that there were two other wives—she didn't know about the children—and in turn and of course as one would expect, Shelly had lost her ever-loving mind, threatening to kill him and those bitches!

What got her was that when she confronted him, he didn't even deny it. When she threatened to tell the world, he fell down on his knees and cried.

Claude confessed that he knew he was sick, a result of his extreme insecurity.

The women meant nothing to him. *She* was the only woman he wanted, the only woman he needed!

He would never go near those other women ever again.

"Cross my heart and swear to god."

Stupidly she believed him and forgave him and a month later, labor pains cutting though her body as she twisted and turned in the hospital bed, Claude came to her with a hefty document. "Baby, I know this isn't the right time, but I need you to sign these."

His attorney stood behind him, his face slowly turning a pale green.

She hadn't even asked what the documents were for. Never in her wildest dreams could she imagine that Claude would pull such a stunt.

Shelly signed everywhere Claude instructed her to and then he signed and then the attorney notarized everything right there in the delivery room.

Shelly found out the news when she was suckling her daughter for the first time. The attorney had come back, sticking his bald head around the green privacy curtain.

"Where's Claude?"

Shelly hadn't expected the attorney to be the first person to come visit her after she gave birth.

The attorney's face was like stone as he handed her a large manila envelope, heavy with documents.

Shelly stretched out her free hand and grabbed hold of the envelope. "Did he have a business meeting to attend?" she asked.

She knew Claude was a very busy, very important man, and so her feelings weren't too badly hurt when she realized nearly a day had gone by since she'd given birth and he hadn't come to visit.

The attorney was tight-lipped. But Shelly didn't miss the flicker of shame in his eyes.

"Good day," he stammered before turning to leave, and then, almost as an afterthought he said, "and congratulations on your beautiful baby."

Shelly shrugged her shoulders and tossed the envelope aside.

Later, after she'd left three messages on Claude's phone, she reached for the envelope and began thumbing through the paperwork.

It began, *"I, Shenelody Miller . . ."*

Shelly read through, with growing horror, the paragraphs upon paragraphs of legal jargon. And with each turn of a page, her vision clouded with tears.

It appeared that she had signed divorce papers and had agreed never to reveal the fact that she had known or even been married to Claude Justine.

The child would not have his last name, but he would support said child until it was an adult.

Apparently Shelly accepted all of these terms along with

one million dollars that had already been deposited into her account.

"Bastard!" Shelly screamed, flinging the papers violently across the room.

She'd taken him to court, of course, but the document was legal and binding and sure, she could try to find loopholes, but that would be near impossible and expensive, her attorney had advised.

"Just take the money, darling," Eloise Shipton had counseled in her Southern drawl, "and start a new life. Forget about him."

It was easier said than done, but she'd done it.

Shelly moved to the West Coast and went back to school. She threw herself into learning and into raising her child. It wasn't until a professor pulled her aside to praise a short story she'd written that Shelly even considered writing as a career.

"You should really think about expanding on this story and submitting it," he'd urged.

And she did just that. Poured all of her love, hate and frustration into that one story.

But as good as her professor claimed her story was, the publishing houses begged to differ, and so she'd gone the self-publishing route.

At first just one hundred copies, which she carried around in her backpack, hawking them to her classmates.

When she sold out of those she had two hundred more copies printed and started leaving those at local bookstores, handing out free copies during rallies, leaving them in conspicuous places.

She received e-mail after e-mail congratulating her on her tantalizing story and inquiring when the next one was coming.

Inspired, she dove into a prequel and then a sequel. All were received well.

A year later, the big boys came knocking, offering her a six-figure book deal. Shelly snubbed her nose at them and they hiked the offer up to seven figures.

It was pure coincidence that she'd ended up living right across the street from Claude. She'd been on the West Coast for nearly fifteen years, but their daughter had made up her mind that she wanted to attend a creative and gifted boarding school in Delaware and so Shelly had packed up and moved back east.

After a stint in New York, she'd finally settled in Plainfield.

Claude came a year later. But due to their hectic travel schedules, neither one knew the other was living on the same street for some time.

In fact they hadn't laid eyes on each other until just a few weeks before Crystal and Javid arrived.

Shelly had laughed herself silly at the look of shock, surprise and anger on his face when their eyes met.

She saw his lips form the word "Fuck!" and all Shelly could think of saying was, "Now is that any way to greet your first wife after all of these years?"

"You were my second wife," he'd hissed at her before climbing into his expensive car and screeching away.

She was surprised to find that his words had stung, even after so many years.

One day, she'd sent her daughter—*their* daughter—over to return a magazine the postman had mistakenly put into her mailbox.

Shelly knew she should have just tossed the magazine away or given it back to the postman, but she was feeling particularly ornery that day and just wanted to see exactly what Claude would do when he came face to face with his daughter.

Claude swung the door open, took the magazine, and thanked Amber as if she was some stranger. As if they didn't share the same bloodline.

His eyes hardly swept her face before he closed the door.

# 31

"*Omigoooooood!*" *Geneva squealed* after flinging the door open and looking out to see Noah, Zahn and their daughter, Destiny.

She ran into Noah's arms and they squeezed each other tight. "I-I can't believe it's you," she blubbered, as she wiped the tears of happiness from her cheeks.

Geneva pulled back and then fell into him again.

"I guess you and I are just chopped liver, Destiny," Zahn quipped in his British accent.

"Oh no, no, of course not!" Geneva announced as she released Noah and went to Zahn, embracing him in a bear hug and then leaning down toward Destiny.

"Aunt Geneva, not so tight this time, okay?"

Geneva waved her hand and scooped the child up into her arms.

It had been more than a year since Geneva had seen them.

She, Noah, Crystal and Chevy had grown up together in the

Manhattan projects. They'd been inseparable up until a few years ago. Noah had started the trend, living part time in London with his lover, Zahn, and then moving there completely after he found he'd fathered a child during the year he'd come to refer to as his year of "madness," when he'd spent twelve full months sleeping with women.

The mother of his daughter was a really nice woman whose life was being torn apart by MS.

"Where's the little woman?" Noah asked as Geneva gave them a quick walk through the new place.

"With her daddy."

Noah was hinting about moving back to the States.

". . . even though it's a shithole of confusion with that damn Bush!"

"Yeah, well, this is his last year and I'm voting for Obama!"

"Me too!" Destiny looked up from her bowl of grapes and yelped.

"Too much BBC and CNN," Zahn whispered.

Destiny, just six years old, was as smart as a twenty-year-old, in Geneva's opinion.

They settled themselves down onto the matching sofa and loveseat. Noah ran his palm across the upholstered material and his face shone with approval. Geneva felt a wave a pride rush through her.

"So you said you didn't tell Crystal you were coming to town?" asked Geneva.

"Well, I told her we were planning to come soon, but I didn't give her an exact date."

Geneva rubbed her hands together. "We should surprise her!"

"My exact thought," Noah concurred. "I really want to meet

this man . . . What's his name again, sweetie?" Noah turned to Zahn.

Zahn shot Noah a bored look as he brushed a lock of blond hair from his face. "It's Claude. How can you forget? She starts every sentence with 'Claude.'"

"It's true." Geneva snickered.

"Yeah, well, she makes him sound like he's God's gift. So do tell, Geneva." Noah folded one leg beneath him and slipped his pinky finger in the corner of his mouth. "Is he?"

Geneva shrugged her shoulders. "Haven't had the pleasure."

"What?"

"I've seen Crystal twice since she's been back. We met for lunch in the city a few times and the other time I went out to her place, but Claude had taken the kids to the Bronx Zoo."

Noah's eyebrows climbed.

"Interesting."

Zahn waved his hand dismissively. "Enough about Crystal's God's gift . . . Where is yours hiding?"

Geneva's sunny mood clouded over. "On tour for a month."

Noah slapped her knee. "Well, I guess that means you'll need extra batteries now, won't you!" he cackled.

"Extra batteries for what, Daddy?" Destiny asked.

"Never you mind," Zahn said as he threw Noah a wicked look.

# 32

Karma's hands were shaking, so she shoved them deeper into the pockets of the trench coat she wore.

"Hello," she said as she approached the front desk. "CJ please."

The front-desk manager, a middle-aged Asian woman, gave her a once-over and then smiled knowingly before picking up the phone and calling Claude's suite.

Of course she knew. It was eighty degrees outside and Karma was wrapped up tight in a navy blue trench coat.

"It's the Cual Flor Penthouse," the manager said, and handed Karma a key.

"Stick this into the slot on the elevator and it will take you straight up."

Karma didn't even offer a word of thanks. She hurried across the floor, her stilettos clicking loudly against the marble as she went. She felt as if the entire hotel could hear her and knew what naughty deed she was off to commit.

"Fuck," she murmured, once inside the safe confines of the elevator. "Karma, girl, you have lost your entire mind," she scolded herself.

The elevator doors slid open, exposing the palatial penthouse suite, which was decorated in different shades of cream and chocolate.

"Hello?" she called as she took a hesitant step into the room. "CJ?"

Beethoven's Symphony no. 5 was gliding from speakers she couldn't see and vapors from a sumptuous scented oil enwrapped her, instantly melting away her anxiety.

She walked toward the glass table, where a chilled bottle of champagne, two flutes and a bowl of chocolate-covered fruit waited.

Karma was about to unknot the belt of her trench coat when CJ's voice floated from the right of her. "No, I want to do that."

Karma swung around.

CJ had changed his mind about greeting her in his birthday suit. Instead he had wrapped himself in the plush terry-cloth robe provided by the hotel.

He started toward her, taking long confident strides.

"So glad you came," he said, resting his hand on her shoulder and pressing a gentle kiss onto her lips.

Karma swooned.

CJ reached over and plucked a strawberry from the bowl. "Do you like strawberries?" he whispered.

Karma's voice had left her. She nodded her head.

"And chocolate?"

Again she nodded her head.

Claude grinned as he slid the tip of the strawberry along her trembling lips until they parted. He took that opportunity to slowly move the strawberry into her mouth, teasing the tip of her tongue.

Karma's eyes fluttered closed and desire swept through her body, causing her to sway in her stilettos.

CJ had no pity for her; he glided one piece of fruit after the next over her lips, across her collarbones, down the center of her neck, deep into her cleavage.

Finally, he undid the belt of her trench coat, parting the panels; he was extremely pleased with what he saw. Removing the coat, he tossed it to the side and slid the thin straps of the teddy off her shoulders.

Karma wanted to be an active participant in their foreplay, but when she raised her arms, he gently moved them back down to her sides.

CJ rolled down the bodice of the teddy, exposing her breasts. He gasped in awe of her pert, full nipples. "Beautiful," he whispered before taking the left, then the right one into his warm mouth.

Karma moaned, and pressed her hands against his shoulder blades.

He sucked with abandon, and the silky seat of her teddy went wet.

CJ reluctantly pulled himself away from her breasts and slid the teddy down, down, until it lay in a silky mound at her feet.

Karma didn't know when he'd disrobed, but when she opened her eyes he was naked and it was her turn to admire him.

CJ's body was flawless, from his smooth chiseled chest to his washboard stomach and muscular thighs.

"Oh my," she gasped as her eyes devoured the gleaming, dark stallion that reached out to her. It'd been a long time since she'd seen a dick that beautiful.

Karma, unable to contain herself, dropped down to her knees and began gently sucking the tip of his manhood.

CJ grunted with pleasure and grabbed hold of her hair.

Karma sucked and licked and rolled her tongue around every inch of his cock, and then she pulled back and leveled a wad of spit on his manhood.

CJ made a sucking sound with his mouth and moaned, "Oh fuck, baby, that shit is so hot."

She swallowed him again, wringing his penis between her palms as she worked her magic with her mouth.

CJ's eyes rolled up into his head and his knees began to falter. No one had sucked his dick like that ever, and even as the thought raced through his mind, he felt the pressure building up in his groin and before he could pull away from her, his back stiffened, his toes curled and he heard himself cry out as he came gushing into her mouth.

He was about to apologize. He was, after all, a gentleman. But when he looked down, Karma was grinning happily up at him, her lips glistening with his seed.

# 33

Crystal was staring at the door, well, really, at the lock on the door.

It couldn't be picked, because it was a combination lock and digital at that.

She'd pressed a number of combinations into the pad . . . his birthday, her birthday, his daughter's birthday, Javid's birthday . . . and still the knob refused to turn.

Crystal knew exactly why she was suddenly bothered by Claude's locked office.

She'd been in that house for three months, passing this very door a hundred times a day and rarely giving it a second glance, but Crystal had had a disturbing dream and woken this morning in a foul mood. She couldn't quite remember the content of the dream, but she did remember that it had involved Claude's office.

That dream, coupled with a comment she'd thought she'd

heard Shelly mumble under her breath, explained why she was standing before it now, not even dressed and company barely thirty minutes away.

She grabbed hold of the knob once more, giving it a violent yank; of course nothing happened. In fact, the door—the knob as well as the combination keypad—seemed to mock her.

"Mommy," Javid called to her from the second-floor landing.

"I'm coming, goddamnit!" she screamed back, before turning and climbing the stairs.

She never spoke to her child that way and she could already hear Javid whimpering in his room.

"How did you two get here?" was all Crystal could think to say when she swung her door open and found Geneva and Karma standing there.

They were supposed to call her when they arrived at the bus stop.

"I can drive, you know," Geneva whined as she tossed a set of car keys from one hand to the next.

Crystal smirked at her. "Whatever," she said, and then looked at Karma and said, "Hey, girl, nice to see you again."

The two women stepped in; Crystal pushed the door forward on its hinges and it bounced back.

"Surprise!" Noah screamed.

Crystal was dumbstruck for a moment. Her eyes went wide, and then her hand came up and covered her mouth in surprise. From where Noah was standing he could clearly see the tears welling up in Crystal's eyes.

"Oh, Miss Thang," he sang, his voice choked with tears. Then when Zahn and Destiny stepped in, the waterworks really got started.

Karma, Zahn and Destiny watched as the three old friends embraced each other and wept.

Eyes red and still sniffling, they gathered in the kitchen.

"I just can't believe you guys are here!"

Crystal had a tight grip on Noah's hand. It didn't seem as if she'd ever let it go.

Looking down at Destiny she exclaimed, "You are getting so big, young lady. You and Javid are making me feel old."

Kayla lurked nearby, clutching her doll and sulking. She didn't quite like it when she wasn't the only pretty little girl in the room.

Noah hoisted himself up onto the wrought-iron stool and lifted Javid onto his knee.

Tweaking his little nose he asked, "Do you want to come to England and stay with your uncle Noah?"

Javid nodded his head enthusiastically.

"Javid, you'd leave me to go with Uncle Noah?"

Javid thought about it for a while and then asked, "Can Mommy come too?"

"I'll have to think about that." Noah laughed before setting him down again.

"Crystal, I know ya'll got a kiddy room for these three to entertain themselves while we talk grown-up," Noah said slyly.

Crystal grinned. She was looking forward to some grown-up talk, some happy reminiscing.

"Ya'll go downstairs to the playroom," Crystal ordered. "I'll bring some sandwiches and juice boxes down in a minute."

Geneva frowned. "Where's your maid?"

Crystal cringed at the word "maid." "She's off sick. Pneumonia, the flu or something like that."

"Well, I know I didn't come all the way out here to eat sandwiches—"

"Don't worry, Geneva," Crystal calmly assured her, "I fried some chicken, made some potato salad and honey-kissed beans."

"Ah, sookie-sookie now!" Geneva squealed with delight.

"So," Noah began, after Crystal rested a loaded plate of food down before him, "where's the man of the house?"

Crystal smiled broadly; the arrival of her friends had sent the dream, the lock and Shelly's words up in smoke. Now she was nothing but happy.

"I expect him shortly," she said as she set Geneva's plate down before her. "He was in California for a few days and should be climbing into his private car right about now." She glanced at the digital clock on the double oven.

"Oooooh, private car," Noah mocked.

"Must be nice to be married to a rich man," Geneva managed between bites of her chicken.

Zahn's head flew up. "You got married?" He turned to Noah. "You said they were shacking up—"

Noah raised his hand, halting Zahn's words in their tracks. He turned and looked at Crystal. "Well, Miss Thang?"

Crystal shook her head in dismay and swatted Geneva on her shoulder. "Of course I didn't marry him—well, not yet. Do you really think I would go and do a thing like that and not say a word, and not invite you to the wedding?"

"I'm saying," Geneva sputtered after taking a large gulp of her Pepsi, "might as well be married. The two of you are living like man and wife."

"So is he as glorious as you've been making him out to be?"

Crystal eased herself down into her chair and blanketed them all with a dreamy look. "He's a wonderful, wonderful man. You know that song by Kimberly Locke . . . he's like that!"

"Kimberly who?" Noah asked.

"Oh, oh . . . I know," Geneva shouted excitedly. "The American Idol girl!"

"You mean," Karma, who had been quiet for the most part, suddenly sprang to life, "the song 'Eighth Wonder'?"

"That's the one!" Crystal clapped her hands together.

That's funny, Karma thought to herself. It was the very same song that had been streaming through her mind since she'd left CJ last night.

" 'Eighth Wonder'?" Zahn had a lost look on his face.

"Yeah, it's such a sweet song—" Crystal started, but Karma interrupted.

"She's singing about being in love with the eighth wonder of the world—which just happens to be her man."

"Awwww," Zahn and Noah cried in unison.

"Karma has a wonderful man too," Geneva happily announced. "But she ain't giving up any info."

"Huh." Karma's head bounced and the expression that appeared on her face resembled that of a child with her hand caught in the cookie jar.

Zahn quipped, "Please, do tell."

The three of them leaned in, their eyes hungry for information.

Karma blushed and stammered, "Well, um, I wouldn't call him my man—"

"Seems they had quite a time at the Pierre Hotel last night," Geneva interrupted.

"The Pierre Hotel," Noah crooned, "veerrry nice. Sounds like he has money?"

"Well, I don't—" Karma started, but Geneva cut her off again.

"Flew her to New Hampshire in his private helicopter."

Karma glared at Geneva.

"Tell it, tell it all, girl." Noah laughed, snapping his fingers.

Crystal crumpled a napkin and threw it across the table at Geneva. Amazingly, it landed right in her mouth.

They all broke down with laughter.

"Serves you right, you and your big-ass mouth," Crystal cried, "telling all of Karma's business like that!"

The joyous uproar continued and so no one heard Claude walk into the kitchen.

"Tell me the joke, I want to laugh too," he said.

# 34

Claude thought he was seeing things and so closed his eyes and willed Karma's face to disappear from the room, but when he re-opened them her shocked expression was still gazing at him.

Crystal had her arms around his neck, her lips pressed into his cheek, and then she had him by the hand pulling him toward the table of strangers and Karma.

She was talking, he could see her lips moving, but he couldn't hear a word she was saying. There was a loud buzzing sound in his ears and it was growing louder.

Claude would later swear that someone had pulled the floor from beneath his feet, and that the earth had opened its mouth and sucked him down into its grimy depths, and then he would re-member the phantom blow to his stomach and how he'd wrenched his hand from Crystal's grip and fled from the room.

He barely made it into the bathroom before the last two meals he'd consumed came tumbling violently from his mouth.

Claude's worlds had finally collided. But how had it happened? He'd been so careful, so fucking careful!

His stomach bubbled, and he braced himself for the next wave of sick.

He'd been too cocky, too sure of himself, too greedy?

Perhaps it was all of these things.

Crystal was at his side, he could see her calves, her beautiful lean calves, and he could hear her worried questions, feel her hand on his shoulder and finally the cool cloth she pressed against his forehead.

"I-I think I ate something bad," he said as she helped him to the bed. "Please apologize to your friends for me," he managed before she slipped his shoes from his feet and pulled the comforter over him.

Back in the kitchen Geneva had already filled the kettle with water and set it on the lit burner.

"Where's your tea?" she said, already opening cabinet doors.

"Peppermint would be best," Zahn added as he stood to help.

"In the, um . . ." Crystal's words trailed off.

"Don't worry, baby, we'll find it," Noah said.

They were treating her as if she was the sick one. She gathered her thoughts and went to the cupboard to retrieve a coffee mug, and that's when she happened to look over at Karma, who was sitting stark still, her eyes wide as saucers and her mouth gaping open.

"You okay, Karma?"

Karma hadn't moved an inch. If she had, her heart, which was galloping a million miles a minute, would have burst from her chest.

"Karma?" Crystal shook the stunned woman's shoulder.

Karma snapped to life. "I have to go," she said, springing from her chair.

"Go?" Noah whirled around, the box of peppermint tea in his hand. "Go where, why?"

Karma snatched her purse from the table. "I have something I need to take care of," she blurted out.

"Since when?" Geneva asked.

Karma didn't have an answer; all she knew was that she couldn't spend one more second in that house, no less an entire night.

"How do you plan on getting home? I know I'm not driving back to the city tonight." Noah was annoyed.

"I'll take a bus, a cab—"

Geneva came and stood before her. "You will not. We came out to have a good time and that's what we're going to do. Now sit your ass down," she said, and gave Karma a light-hearted shove toward the chair.

Karma wanted to leap at her and scratch her eyes out. But she controlled the rage inside of her and sat down. "I just thought with, with your—"

"Claude," Crystal said, giving Karma a wary look.

"Yes, Claude being sick, I just don't think that we . . . I mean, I should stay. I'm sure he needs all of your attention right about now."

She gulped on the last few words. She wanted to cry so bad it hurt. What a fool, what a goddamn fool she was!

This man, this Claude, CJ, whatever the hell he called himself, had a good life and a good woman. How could he have done and said all of those things last night?

"It's okay, Karma, really it is," Crystal said before heading back up the stairs to Claude.

Noah considered Karma for a minute before scooting close to her and asking, "Honey girl, is it that time of the month?"

Claude lay in a fetal position. Waiting. He fully expected Karma to blurt out everything. Every goddamn thing!

Women and their mouths. Their goddamn filthy mouths! Claude punched the pillow.

He could just leave. He could get up and just walk right out of his house. Right out of Crystal's life. He'd done it before. It hadn't been hard.

When Kayla's mother, Denise, started acting crazy, talking madness, accusing him of all sorts of things, telling him that her ancestors had come to her in her dreams and told her of his infidelity, he knew it was time to cut and run.

And he'd done just that, but not before he admitted her into a psychiatric hospital.

Kayla was a little more than a year old then, and after a few months she stopped asking for her mother, and Claude simply moved to another part of the state and told people who inquired that Denise had died.

Simple.

But now as he lay curled into a ball of anxiety he wondered if Denise's final words to him had magically come true: "Karma, Claude, karma! She's a bitch and one day she will have your balls for dinner!"

Claude reached down between his legs and protectively cupped his testicles.

# 35

Crystal was no longer having a good time as she tried to split herself between her friends and her sick husband.

Up and down the steps she went. Checking on Claude every fifteen minutes.

"Can you just tell them to go?" he pleaded. "I really need you to be with me."

It wasn't an outrageous request, and she knew that it was probably the best thing to do, but Zahn, Noah and Geneva had already gone through three bottles of wine and none of them was in any condition to get on the road.

Although she didn't know whether Karma drove, she hadn't had a drop to drink. In fact, she hadn't uttered more than two words since Geneva had bullied her back into her chair.

It was all very odd. Very, very odd.

They all turned in about three that morning.

Crystal walked into the bedroom and was surprised to find Claude sitting on the edge of the bed, his head in his hands.

She went to him. "Maybe we should go to the hospital?"

He shook his head no.

"I'll be fine. Are they all asleep?"

Crystal yawned. "Asleep, no. Passed out, yes," she said as she climbed into bed. Within a few minutes she was snoring.

Thank goodness Crystal had put her on the pull-out sofa in her office. Karma couldn't have beared being down the hall from their bedroom. Not that being beneath their bedroom was a good thing, but it was better than the alternative.

She tossed and turned on the thin mattress, her mind dragging her back to the day they met. Some bells should have gone off. Sirens. Something!

She'd known about Sergio's women, why hadn't it been obvious with Claude?

Now wait a minute, her mind cautioned, you never even asked the man if he was single, you just assumed.

Karma sat bolt upright.

But he'd taken her to his home in New Hampshire, and just last night when they were together he suggested that they fly down to Orlando for a few days next month around the eighteenth or so . . .

He said he had some business meetings, but would put aside time for them.

Them.

He said it like they were an item and Karma had transformed that into US.

Karma swung her legs from the bed and set her feet down onto the floor. She should march right up those stairs, she told herself, barge right into their bedroom and tell Crystal everything!

What would he do? Deny it?

Let him try, she fumed, she had a love bite on her breast that perfectly matched his teeth.

We could go to the dentist right now, Crystal, if you need further proof!

Karma gave her head a violent shake. Now she was thinking crazy!

Claude eased himself from the bed, out of the room and down the staircase.

He didn't know what he was going to do or say, he just knew he had to see her. Confront her.

He moved silently across the Berber carpet, and then across the marble floor of the hallway toward Crystal's office.

The door was shut and he stood there for a moment, staring at the dark oak of the door while his heart clamored in his chest.

After some time he reached out and curled his sweaty palm around the brass doorknob.

Karma was standing by the window, staring out at the lonely street when the door swung open. She yelped in surprise when the dark figure rushed her.

"Shhhhh." Claude wrapped one arm around her waist and he used his free hand to cover her mouth.

"Don't you scream," he ordered.

Karma struggled, but she was no match for his strength.

"Promise you won't scream. Promise," Claude insisted.

Karma nodded her head.

"You son of a bitch!" she spat and slapped him across his face when he finally released her.

Claude said nothing.

"You lied to me!"

Claude smirked. "I did no such thing, Karma. You never asked about my availability," he said smugly. "And I didn't ask you about yours."

Karma raised her hand to slap him again, but he caught her by the wrist and pulled her roughly to him.

"You wanted to fuck me and I wanted to fuck you and so we both got what we wanted, didn't we?"

Karma wrenched herself from his grip.

"You women, you all want to play the game and make rules as you go along. But that's not how it works."

Karma glared at him. She didn't know what the fuck he was talking about.

"Now," he continued as he sat down on the edge of the desk and folded his arms across his chest, "what are your plans?"

"What?" Karma didn't know what he was talking about.

"C'mon, Karma, you're an intelligent woman. You've had more than a few hours to think about how you're going to try and get back at me. Make me feel the hurt that you're feeling now."

Karma felt like she was in the twilight zone. She couldn't believe that she was standing in her lover's house having this conversation while his soon-to-be wife was fast asleep in the room right above their heads.

"You're fucking crazy, you know that!"

"Am I?"

Claude reached for her, catching hold of the flimsy material of her nightgown. He yanked her to him and grabbed her head; holding it tight, he pressed a rough kiss onto her lips.

Karma fought against his probing tongue until her resolve seeped from her body.

Claude pulled back. "I want you and I know you want me. This doesn't have to change anything, we could go on like this forever."

Karma started to respond, but he pressed his mouth against her again and then suddenly, during some strange maneuver she would never be able to conceive, her breasts were out and his mouth was on them, hot and hungry, sucking savagely at her nipples.

Karma flung her head back in ecstasy. Claude's hands were everywhere, like tentacles, and then his fingers were up inside of her, probing, pushing, and all the while she moaned, "No, no, we can't," while she pulled him closer.

He spun her around, bent her over the desk, and began biting into her back. Karma's body began to tremble with hot pleasure.

"Claude—" she whispered breathlessly as he violently tore her panties from her body and without warning rammed himself deep inside of her.

Karma cried out in surprise, and that was the last audible sound she made until he was done with her. Claude had clamped his palm tightly over her mouth, muffling her cries. The fingers of his other hand dug deep into her shoulder blade, holding her steady as he pounded mercilessly into her.

The danger of it all made Claude feel powerful, made him dizzy with it.

"Fuck, fuck, fuck," he whispered with each angry thrust.

Karma tried to buck him off, but Claude dug his fingers deeper into her flesh and continued to ram away. He came with a shuddering grunt and immediately yanked himself out of her and used the hem of her nightgown to wipe his dick clean.

Karma, still bent across the desk, was gulping for air, her eyes slowly filling with shameful tears.

Claude didn't say a word; he just turned and walked out of the room, pulling the door shut behind him.

# 36

"Hey, baby," Crystal greeted Claude, who was stepping out of the shower. "Feeling better?"

Claude placed a quick kiss on her cheek. "Much," he said as he strolled out of the bathroom and toward his wardrobe closet.

Crystal followed him. "Wow, that was a quick recovery," she stated, a bit baffled.

"Uh-huh," Claude sounded as he hit the switch that rotated the clothing racks.

Crystal shrugged her shoulders. "I guess it was a twenty-four-hour thing then, huh?"

"I guess," Claude responded absently as he reached for a pair of khakis.

Crystal watched him. "Well, I guess Superman ain't got nothing on you, huh?" she muttered as she turned and headed back into the bathroom.

"Not a motherfucking thing," Claude happily sang beneath his breath.

## "Pancakes?"

Javid's and Kayla's heads bounced in agreement.

"Morning." Crystal yawned as she walked into the kitchen. "What's all this?"

"Your man," Noah started in his best Come Back L'il Sheba voice, "is making breakfast. Keep him, girl, keep him!"

"While you were up there primping we've been getting to know each other, haven't we, Claude?" Noah batted his eyes at Claude.

"Yep!"

"You've got a hell of a man here, Crystal," Zahn offered between bites of his turkey bacon. "Any man that makes pancakes like this and is willing to share some of the wealth, is okay in my book."

"Share some of the wealth?" Crystal was confused.

"Stock tips, baby," Claude said, and then, "Do you want some pancakes?"

Crystal grinned. "Sure, why not." Claude poured her a cup of coffee and set it down before her. Crystal took a sip and then asked, "We got two people missing. Where's Karma and Geneva?"

Noah huffed, "You know Geneva ain't getting up before noon, unless of course you have a way to waft the scent of the food upstairs and into her room. That'll get her up!"

"And I think I heard the shower running in the bathroom in your office," Zahn said.

A few minutes later Karma appeared at the doorway of the kitchen.

She hadn't slept a wink and it showed. She immediately unraveled upon finding that the first thing her eyes fell on was Claude's polo-covered back. She almost turned and ran. But she'd come this far, and Noah had assured her that she'd be back in Brooklyn by midday.

"Morning."

She'd spoken so softly that they hadn't heard her above their own chatter.

"Morning," she said again a bit louder.

"Morning," they all turned and responded.

Claude waited a beat and then he turned around and gave her a broad smile. "Hello, you must be Karma," he said as he rounded the island and made his approach.

Karma fought hard to keep the smile on her face in place.

"So sorry about last night." He extended his hand and for a moment all Karma could do was stare at it.

Claude continued, "But I'm much better now." He seemed to loom stories high. "So nice to meet you. Did you sleep well?"

Shelly was still laughing when the sun climbed high into the sky.

It seemed to her that Claude had not changed one single bit!

He'd gotten so bad that he was bringing women home and fucking them right under Crystal's nose.

What a louse. What a trifling, good-for-nothing louse!

She hadn't been to sleep. Sleep didn't even occur to her after she witnessed the scene that took place across the street.

When she slipped the strap of the binoculars around her neck that night, she wasn't expecting much. Crystal led a pretty mundane life. And besides, although their homes faced each other, the only rooms Shelly had been able to infiltrate were the bedroom—and that was only during the day, when Crystal opened the blinds—and the office, whose blinds Crystal never closed.

Shelly had watched her sitting at her computer reading e-mails and talking on the phone, but little else.

She laughed at the irony of it all.

If one of her neighbors were watching her the way she was watching Claude and Crystal, they'd catch her in some compromising positions, and not always with another person.

Last night had more than made up for the weeks of boredom.

It hadn't been her intention to spy on them. Shelly had been working into the wee hours on her manuscript. She'd finally decided to call it a night; switching off the desk lamp, she stood and, like always, peeked through her shutters to give the streets a once-over before she retired to her bedroom.

Her eyes happened to fall on Claude's house, and in the darkness of Crystal's office, she saw movement.

She looked at the clock on her desk. It was almost four in the morning.

Shelly reached for her binoculars, and lo and behold, who did she see bent across that expensive wooden desk, taking it from behind (and Shelly had assumed anally) like an inmate . . . none other than Karma Jackson!

She knew there was something about that girl that didn't quite sit well with her.

And who was doling out the punishment?

Survey says:

Claude Justine!

"God," Shelly cried out to her office walls, "I wish I'd gotten that on videotape!"

# 37

Karma was silent for the entire ride back to New York. Geneva didn't have much to say either; she was nursing a wicked hangover.

Karma gave them all a tight hug and bid them goodbye, and then watched while the rented Charger slowly pulled away from the curb and disappeared down the quiet Brooklyn street.

Up in her apartment she made a beeline toward her bathroom, stripping out of her clothes as she went.

Turning the shower on full blast, she stood beneath the pounding water and cried. She felt dirty and cheap.

How could she have done something so horrible? Fucking a man in his house with his woman just feet away?

And how he'd taken her! Like she was some West Side Highway whore!

Karma reached for the loofah and began roughly scrubbing her skin.

But she'd allowed it. She'd welcomed it! She was a willing participant!

She could have said no, could have screamed and woken up everybody in the house, exposing him for what and who he was!

And what was that exactly?

Karma searched for the proper response.

A dog?

And so what did that make her?

"His bitch," she whispered into the spray of water.

"Geneva, what's up with your girl?" Noah asked as he came to a red light.

Geneva moaned, "What?"

"Karma. What's up with her?"

Yes, she realized that Karma had behaved a bit strangely, but what did Noah expect? He, Zahn and Crystal were all new to her.

"What do you mean?"

"I'm just surprised that she came back to New York after what happened between her and that man she had."

Geneva was perplexed. Geneva had shared the fact that Karma used to be Mildred and that a man had taken her for her life savings, promised to marry her and then left her waiting at the altar. Well, at City Hall.

She'd also told him that after Karma's transformation, the two had met up again in Barbados and the louse didn't even recognize her.

Karma had gone on to seduce him, making him fall in love with her the same way she'd fallen in love with him, and then left him at the altar.

That's as much as Geneva knew.

"Why wouldn't she?"

Noah turned all the way around and gave Geneva a penetrating stare. " 'Cause she took him for damn near a half a million dollars!"

Geneva waved her hand at him. "You don't know what you're talking about. You must still be drunk."

"I know what the hell I'm talking about because I'm the one who helped her do it!"

Geneva stared blankly at him, and then she started to laugh.

Zahn shot a wary look at Geneva but said nothing.

Car horns blasted behind them and Noah threw them the finger before screeching off.

"Chevy called me and told me that she needed me to act as the father of this Karma girl." His words came out in rapid bursts. "To tell this man of hers that I played the currency market and how I could double his money in no time, and just like that the guy transfers two hundred thousand to my account and I in turn transferred it to Karma's account."

Geneva's laughter began to fade. She realized that Noah was dead serious.

"I guess she didn't remember that it was me Chevy called, 'cause she didn't say anything and I certainly wasn't going to mention it."

Karma had never shared any of that with Geneva, and now she sat there dumbfounded.

"You mean she never told you?" Noah asked.

Geneva shook her head.

"Wow." Noah sighed as he pulled the car up in front of Geneva's house. "Well, you ain't hear it from me."

# 38

Shelly waited until the sedan that Claude had climbed into was well out of sight before she opened her front door and stepped outside.

Crystal was still standing on the lawn, a forlorn look on her face as she stared down the road.

"Hey!" Shelly called brightly. "How ya'll doing?" she said, making sure she stayed on her side of the street.

After her visit to the house and Claude's phone call, she'd received a warning letter from Claude's attorney, reminding her of the stipulations of their divorce. She had to remain five hundred feet away from Claude and/or his home.

"Hey, hey." She waved frantically. She wanted Crystal to come over to her side of the street.

Crystal gave her an odd look and then said, "You wanna come over and have a cup of coffee with me?"

"Why don't you come over here," Shelly yelled back. "I have a new cappuccino machine I need to break in."

Again, Crystal shot her an odd look. "Um, it would be best if you came over here, the kids are still in bed. I can't leave them alone in the house."

"Oh, they'll be okay." Shelly knew as soon as the words came out of her mouth that they sounded wrong.

Wasn't she a mother? How could she suggest a woman leave two young children in a house alone, even for a minute. Anything could happen.

Shelly hurried to correct her faux pas. "You're . . . you're right," she said, bobbing her head up and down like some idiot. "I-I have a conference call coming through in a few minutes anyway," she lied. "Maybe we can go to the park later on?"

Crystal's face brightened. "I would like that."

Claude felt like he'd been doing push-ups for two days straight, that's how pumped up he felt.

Power was an amazing thing, he mused as the black sedan sped down Route 22.

He'd done some wild shit; he'd taken his share of chances, but had never come close to screwing another woman right under the nose of one of his main women.

He'd had a hard-on for the rest of the weekend. He could tell by the look on Crystal's face that she was more than happy to see him leave.

Claude had pounced on her every chance he got. And with every stroke, he relived those stolen moments. Even as he reminisced his dick began to stiffen. Sure, he'd taken a wife on vacation and flown a girlfriend down to the same island at the same

time, but he'd always kept the women in separate resorts, and neither one was ever the wiser.

That had made him feel powerful, but now those experiences
seemed like a neophyte's compared to what he'd done over the
weekend.

The rush had been mind-boggling. He couldn't stop thinking
about it. He was like a dope fiend, and even though one part of his
brain was telling him to forget, to store the memory away in the
dark part of his psyche, the other part of his mind, the part that
thrived on living dangerously, was already plotting and scheming
as to just how he could manage to pull it off one more time.

# 39

Joshua Lieberman had been standing over Karma's desk for a full one hundred and twenty seconds before she even sensed he was there.

"Oh, sorry, sir, did you call me?"

Joshua nodded his head. He had called her a number of times from the doorway of his office, and then after she didn't respond he moved closer and closer until he was at her desk, hovering over her.

He actually hadn't really minded standing there; the low-cut blouse she wore treated him to an eyeful of her sexy cleavage, which is why he was flushed in the face when she finally looked up at him.

Joshua cleared his throat and quickly averted his eyes. "Yes, I need you to, um . . ." He trailed off. He'd suddenly forgotten what it was he wanted to say to her.

Damn her breasts!

"Never mind," he mumbled. Embarrassed, he turned and walked away.

Karma shrugged her shoulders listlessly. She didn't know what his problem was. She had her own problems.

The message Geneva left on her voice mail two days earlier was haunting her like a bad dream.

"Karma, I know what you did. We need to talk," she said tersely.

Karma had been nauseous ever since. She was sure Geneva knew about her and Claude and wanted to confront her.

But how did she know?

Karma ran everything round and round in her head and couldn't figure out how it was Geneva knew. She shook her head in dismay. She'd really fucked things up, hadn't she?

And on top of that, she hadn't heard from Claude. She hated herself for wanting to hear from him. She hated that she checked her cell phone every ten minutes, not to mention her e-mail. And she almost jumped out of her chair when her private line at work rang.

But it was never him.

She told herself that that was a good thing, that she should simply pick herself up, brush herself off, forget about Claude and the awful thing they'd done the other night, and move on with her life.

But in her heart she knew that she wouldn't.

# 40

"Mind your business, Geneva," Deeka warned from his hotel suite in Copenhagen. "Stay out of it."

She'd shared everything that Noah had told her, and the fact that she was furious.

" 'Neva, you're being ridiculous. Just because you're friends doesn't mean she has to tell you everything—"

"Says you." Geneva was being stubborn. "Me, Noah and Crystal tell each other everything!"

"If that's true," Deeka sighed, "and God, I hope it's not—"

"What?"

"I'm saying that some things that happen between a man and his wife should stay between a man and his wife."

Geneva rolled her eyes.

"But back to what I was saying, you, Crystal and Noah practically go back to the womb. You've known Karma what, all of two years?"

Geneva grunted.

"And I realize that you failed to include Chevy on your list of complete confidants. Even I know Chevy doesn't tell you guys all of her business."

"Well," Geneva snapped, "Chevy has always been sneaky and—"

"Okay, Geneva, I know I'm not going to win here, so let's just drop it. I called to see how you and Charlie are doing. I really don't have any interest in the *As the World Turns* drama of your friends."

Geneva started to shoot back "Then you don't have any interest in me!"

But thought better of it.

"Okay, Deeka," she said sweetly. "I miss you, baby . . ."

"So I see you had company over the weekend?" Shelly probed as nonchalantly as she could. "That must have been nice."

They were in the park watching the children play.

"Yeah," Crystal said as she crossed her legs. "I left you a message, I wanted you to join us."

"Yes, yes, I got that. But I was out and about all day."

"Really?" Crystal made a face. "Your Mercedes was in the drive—"

"So tell me," Shelly quickly interrupted, "who all came to visit?"

"Oh, Geneva, who you already know, and my friend Noah and his mate Zahn and their—"

"Did Karma come too?" Shelly shot eagerly.

Crystal gave her an odd look. "Yes, as a matter of fact she did," she responded slowly.

Shelly seemed to be waiting for something else.

"We sat around drinking wine and talking shit, you know, the usual."

Shelly was rapidly nodding her head, and Crystal got the impression that she wanted to hurry up to the good part. But Crystal didn't know what the good part was.

"Um, then Claude came home."

Shelly's body jerked and she straightened her back.

"He was sick so he really didn't get to spend any time with them until the following morning."

Sick? He looked perfectly healthy when he was using his dick as a battering ram on Karma.

Shelly was flabbergasted. Crystal really had no clue.

"What?"

"Nothing, girl, nothing."

Crystal's face went blank and then suddenly lit up. She wagged her index finger at Shelly. "Are you fishing for material for your next book?"

Shelly figured it was best to play along and grinned sheepishly. "Yeah."

"I knew it!"

# 41

Claude pulled the phone from his ear and stared at it for a moment before pressing it back and asking, "I lost how much?"

His broker, Sal, a sharp Latino from the Dominican Republic, cleared his throat before repeating himself: "Forty-two million dollars."

Claude's heart dropped down into his stomach. He'd taken hits before, but never anything like this.

"Claude, the market, you know how it goes."

Claude did know, but forty-two million dollars?

"You're my watchdog, Sal, why weren't you watching?"

Sal was glad he was in his office in New York City, so that Claude couldn't see him flipping him the bird.

Sal wasn't really the watchdog. Claude had always done his own watching, his own watching and his own picking—he just called Sal to make the transactions.

All Sal could think of to say was, "Everybody got hit, Claude, some harder than others. You'll bounce back and—"

It took a moment before Sal realized he was consoling dead air.

By the time Claude's sedan pulled into the private community of Privada, located in North Scottsdale, Arizona, twilight had already fallen over the city. In this luxury community, Claude owned a spacious, one-level Spanish-style home. This house was a favorite of his; the open-plan living and glass walls brought the outside in.

Claude let himself into the house and the bull mastiff, Jake, bounded from the kitchen and met him at the door.

"Hey, boy, hey," Claude said as he roughly scratched the large canine behind his ears. "Where's mama, where's mama, huh?"

Jake bounded down the glass-walled corridor toward the master bedroom.

Pryor was early to bed and early to rise. The only one of his wives who would never bear him children—a childhood disease had rendered her barren.

Long and luscious Pryor, so dark, her nickname was Chocolate.

Pryor spent her late teens and early twenties walking the catwalks of Paris and gracing the glossy pages of fashion magazines before she decided to become an artist. The two had met at an exhibition of hers. Claude dropped a cool twenty thousand dollars on one of her landscapes, and Pryor agreed to go out on a date with him.

Three months later he slipped a two-carat ring on her finger, and three months after that they became man and wife.

Because of her inability to have children, Pryor was overly grateful to have Claude. She still found it unbelievable that this man of such means couldn't care less about her producing an heir; all that mattered, he reiterated each and every time they were together, was the love they had for each other.

Claude walked into the kitchen, opened the refrigerator and retrieved a bottle of sparkling water. Twisting off the cap, he tilted his head and drank deeply.

He would spend tomorrow going over his investments. He had to admit he'd not been as diligent as usual. His extracurricular activities were starting to impinge on his money and that wasn't a good thing.

Setting the empty bottle down onto the blue-and-silver-flecked granite countertop, he started toward the bedroom.

When Jake saw him coming he rose and began panting happily as he wagged his bobbed tail.

Claude made a quick sweeping motion with his hand and Jake obediently trotted off to another part of the house.

Claude pushed the door open and stepped into the darkness of the room. He gently pulled the door closed behind him.

Soft music swirled around the room. Pryor liked to go to sleep to music. But above the music he heared giggling and moans.

His hand went immediately to the light switch and what he saw was Pryor, her long chocolate legs thrown over the white shoulders of a person whose head was planted deep between her thighs.

"What the fuck!" Claude's voice shattered the night, and Jake's barking followed.

"Oh God, Claude!" Pryor screamed.

"What the fuck!" Claude yelled again, his hands balled into tight fists!

The head between Pryor's legs quickly dislodged itself and turned and looked up at Claude.

Claude knew the face.

"Megan?"

It was Pryor's personal trainer.

"Now, Claude, let me explain." Pryor's words shot rapidly from her mouth.

"Ya'll fucking each other?" Claude felt the room begin to spin. He stepped up to Pryor, who had leaped from the bed, and grabbed her roughly by the throat. "You're a fucking lesbo?"

Before he knew it, Megan had come from behind Pryor and punched him hard on the side of his head.

Jake was at the door, barking and butting his head against the closed door like he'd gone mad.

Claude grabbed his head and stumbled sideways—that's when Megan hit him again, this time two quick assaults to his midsection and then the knock-out punch, a sharp uppercut to his chin.

When Claude came to, Pryor, Jake and Megan were gone. She'd taken most of her wardrobe, but had left the BMW and the jewelry he'd bought her over the years.

And there was a note:

> Claude,
> Sorry you had to find out this way.
> Pryor

Claude eased himself down onto the edge of the king-size bed and stared at the note. After a long moment he began to laugh. He shook his finger first at the note and then at the heavens.

It was at that moment that Claude realized he was getting a spiritual whoop-ass. His life was slowly unraveling. It made perfect sense; he'd become greedy and sloppy in his affairs. This was all bound to happen.

Claude rose from the bed and started down the corridor toward the front door. He would take a break. Maybe spend a month or two in one of his five beach homes around the world. All he needed was a little time to recoup, reevaluate and reenergize himself. He'd come back stronger, smarter and richer.

Karma wasn't going to have his balls for dinner, he thought as he walked out into the sunlit morning, not even for an appetizer.

three days later

# 42

Crystal rubbed the heels of her hands together. Her stomach was queasy and she felt like she was going to keel over at any moment.

It had been three days since she'd heard from Claude. That wasn't like him. When he traveled he called at least twice a day to check up on them.

She paced the house. Not sure exactly what it was she should do.

All types of horrors passed through her mind. She'd been watching the news and hadn't heard about any air disasters, but maybe he'd been killed in a car accident, maybe he'd been kidnapped!

Crystal rushed to the front door and flung it wide open on its hinges and dashed across the street, barely missing getting hit by an oncoming Volkswagen bug.

"Shelly!" she yelled as she pounded on the front door. "Shelly!"

Shelly came out of the garage. "Crystal?"

Babbling incoherently, Crystal rushed to her and grabbed hold of her wrist, frantically jerking her toward her house.

Shelly jerked back. "What's wrong, what's happening?"

Crystal was inconsolable and the only word Shelly was able to make out was "Claude."

"Something happened to Claude?"

Crystal nodded her head and composed herself long enough to say, "I don't know what to do."

Shelly followed her to the house and took a hesitant step over the door's threshold. Crystal turned pleading eyes on her; Shelly took a deep breath and followed her inside.

In the living room, they sat alongside each other, thighs pressed together as Shelly calmed Crystal down to a level where she could understand exactly what was upsetting her.

Crystal brushed at her tears and explained to Shelly that she hadn't heard from Claude in three days and she knew in her gut that something was terribly wrong, because this behavior was unlike him.

Shelly listened intently.

"If I report him missing, they'll want a snapshot, but I don't have one because . . ."

And the flood of tears came on again.

After Crystal had explained why it was she had no pictures of Claude, Shelly just stared at her.

"Shelly?"

Shelly let out a long, exasperated sigh. Claude had come a long way; his snow jobs had grown into full-scale blizzards.

"Crystal," Shelly began as she squeezed her knee, "don't worry. I have a picture of him."

Crystal's head snapped up.

"What? How . . ."

Shelly rose from the sofa. "I have an entire album of pictures of him. Albeit, they're about eighteen years old, but he still looks pretty much the same," she said as she started toward the door.

"Call the police and I'll tell you the whole story when I get back."

Crystal watched Shelly's retreat in quiet amazement. "I must be dreaming," she muttered, and then took hold of the fatty part of her arm and pinched, hard.

The pain cut through her.

Yep, she was awake.

# 43

Karma set her plate of sushi on the coffee table, reached for the remote and turned on the television.

She was surfing through channels when her cell phone began to vibrate. She looked at the number; it was Geneva, again.

"Get a fucking life," she murmured, and flung the phone to the other end of the couch.

Geneva had called her a total of six times since Monday. She'd left three messages, and with each message her tone became more and more severe.

Karma thought about just calling her, waiting for her hello and then screaming, "Yes, I fucked your friend's boyfriend!" and being done with the whole sordid mess.

But she hadn't summoned the nerve to do so yet.

She had, however, broken down and called Claude. Karma had tossed "CJ" aside, now that she knew his full name.

She felt like a fool every time she dialed his number, and

couldn't believe that the whiney, pleading, tearful messages she left on his voice mail were actually coming out of her mouth.

It had slowly dawned on her that Mildred Johnson wasn't dead at all; she was alive, well and pulsating right beneath her skin.

Karma settled on the evening news, dropped the remote, and was about to reach for her chopsticks when a photograph of Claude flashed across her plasma screen.

Karma sat transfixed; the chopsticks slipped from her hand and clattered down onto the table.

"Girl, I just saw the news!" Geneva screamed from her duplex in Brooklyn. "What the hell is going on?"

Crystal's voice was hoarse.

When Shelly came back with not one but two photo albums filled with pictures of her and Claude, Crystal almost fainted.

Calmly, methodically, Shelly unraveled a very normal boy-meets-girl story that slowly transformed into a horror show.

Crystal kept shaking her head no. But Shelly ripped a Polaroid picture from one of the albums and shoved it in her face. "It's true!"

There'd been yelling, screaming, fits of sobbing, and Crystal had even broken a few decorative figurines.

By the time the police arrived, reality had hit her like a jack-hammer, numbing every molecule of her body, and Crystal, dazed and limp, slumped down onto the couch.

"I know just as much as you do. Which is practically nothing," Crystal whispered hoarsely into the phone to Geneva.

# 44

Have you seen this man?

Millionaire businessman A. Claude Justine has been miss-ing for three days. He was last seen leaving his home in Plain-field, New Jersey.

Mr. Justine told his live-in girlfriend, Crystal Atkins, that he was going to attend a business conference in Chicago.

Channel Seven news contacted the conference organizer and spokesperson, who advised us that no one by the name of Claude Justine ever registered for the conference.

Foul play has not been ruled out. If you have any information on this man, please contact the Plainfield Police Department.

More at 11 o'clock.

Crystal opened the door and tried to read the faces of the two police officers who stood facing her.

"Ma'am, can we come in, please?"

Crystal almost screamed, *"Do you have to come in to tell me he's dead!"*

She stepped aside.

Shelly was in the kitchen with Elvie preparing dinner for the children.

Shelly had promised that she would remain by Crystal's side, no matter how long it took to locate Claude.

"Please sit down," Crystal said.

The officers sat. They looked almost identical; both had close-cropped blond hair and bright blue eyes. The shorter of the two peeled open the manila envelope he carried and pulled out six photographs.

"Do you know any of these women?" he asked as he handed the photos over to Crystal.

Crystal flipped through the photos. She noted that they were all beautiful. "No," she said, and handed the photos back to the officer. "What do these women have to do with Claude?"

The officers exchanged a cautious glance. "Well," the other officer started, "these women all claim to be Claude Justine's wives."

"What?" Shelly screeched from the corner of the room.

Crystal's eyes popped. "All of them?"

"Yes, ma'am, every single last one," he stated emphatically. "They live all around the country. One in New Hampshire, another in Los Angeles, and—"

Crystal pushed her fist into her mouth and raised her free hand. She just couldn't hear any more. How could this nightmare get any worse?

# 45

Karma didn't go to work the next day or the day after that. She seriously doubted that she would ever return to Lieberman and Lieberman, or to the outside world for that matter.

She lay in bed wondering what exactly was wrong with her. Whatever it was, men like Tony and Claude had the exceptional ability to see it and then take advantage of it.

And even now as she tried to escape him, she couldn't; his picture was everywhere, on the television, in the newspaper. Goddammit, he'd even made the back of the milk carton!


Her girl was in trouble, so Geneva paid eighty dollars to a gypsy cabbie to drive her from Brooklyn to Plainfield.

"You know you my girl!" she said when Crystal fell into her arms.

· · ·

Was there no end to the humiliation?

When Crystal was unable to provide any information, other than Claude's physical attributes, the police officers used a battering ram on Claude's office door.

What they found was a computer devoid of its innards and a desk that was empty except for a blank envelope that contained one thin slip of paper.

The officer read the letter, shook his head and then passed it on to his commander, who frowned before handing it to Crystal.

Shelly and Geneva crowded around her.

Crystal, if you're reading this that means that you're not obedient, nor are you trustworthy.
Claude

For a long time Crystal just stared at the words on the paper. Shelly and Geneva braced themselves for the hurricane of emotion that they were sure would come, but instead, Crystal let go a tiny yelp, more like a hiccup really. And then a string of giggles spilled from her and before any of them knew it, Crystal was clutching her side; roaring with laughter.

All over the country the doors to Claude's private home offices were being battered down and searched. The findings were always the same.

· · ·

Claude's wives were making the talk-show rounds. *Ellen, Oprah, The View.*

Their faces were splashed across hundreds of rag-mags around the world. Other women even began to come forward claiming to be wives of A. Claude Justine, and the list of baby mamas grew longer every day.

The Claude Justine saga even overshadowed Britney Spears and her outlandish escapades and, as when any spoiled child realizes that the world has stopped paying them any mind, Britney finally pulled herself together and began acting like she had some goddamn sense.

thirty days later

# 46

Crystal refused to have any part of the media circus swirling around her.

Television and radio producers called her day and night, attempting to lure her with promises of money and expensive gifts. When she couldn't take it anymore, she packed up and high-tailed it to Brooklyn, hiding out at Geneva's place until the media's attention shifted elsewhere.

Now they sat huddled on the couch, clutching their coffee cups and hushing one another as Matt Lauer of the *Today* show reappeared on the television screen.

His guests this morning were Denise Justine and her daughter, Kayla.

Matt leaned back into his chair and crossed his legs. "Before we went to commercial break, you were sharing with the world the life you had with the missing millionaire Claude Justine."

"I don't call it a life, Matt; I refer to it as an ordeal."

Matt nodded his head thoughtfully.

"Your story starts out very similar to the other women in Claude Justine's life. You meet this wonderful man who wines and dines you, you fall in love, get married, have a baby, acquire the big house, luxury car and dog. For all intents and purposes you were living the American dream, until, of course, you discovered that you were bipolar."

Denise looked dead into the camera; the top lid of her right eye twitched continuously. "I was diagnosed with bipolar disorder a year after Claude had me committed."

Now it was Matt's turn to look into the camera.

"Claude Justine had Denise committed to a psychiatric hospital and assumed sole custody of their daughter, Kayla." Matt used his pen to point at Kayla, who hadn't taken her eyes off of the camera.

Turning his focus back to Denise, he said, "And told Kayla and anybody who asked that you were . . . well, that you were dead."

"Yes, that's right, Matt."

"How was it that you were able to regain custody of Kayla?"

"Well, we do have televisions in the crazy house," Denise said with a little laugh. It was a weak attempt at being humorous that failed miserably. "And when I saw that he was missing I knew that this was my chance to finally see my daughter again—"

"Now wait a minute, you had no idea where your daughter was. You didn't know if Claude had kept her or given her away, am I right?"

Denise nodded her head. "I spoke to my psychiatrist and he placed the call to the Plainfield Police Department and—"

Matt hastily interrupted her, "And they in turn found out that your daughter was indeed living in Plainfield with yet another wife—"

Denise raised her hand. "No, Matt, Crystal had not married Claude, they were just living together."

Matt looked closely at his notes.

"Because Claude Justine is a high-profile businessman, the FBI became involved and quickly determined that it wasn't a kidnapping, nor is Claude Justine dead.

"And why is that?" Matt asked before laying one of his penetrating looks on Denise.

"Because the mortgages on all the homes the other so-called wives lived in were paid off and the deeds hand-delivered to them."

"Claude would have had to order this, no?"

Denise nodded.

"But you were in a clinic. Do you have a house?"

Denise shifted uncomfortably in her chair. "I'm currently fighting his attorney for possession of the Plainfield estate," she said.

Crystal laughed. "Estate?"

"I'm also told that each wife received sizable deposits into their individual bank accounts. Did you receive any money?"

Denise glowered at him. "Matt, I was locked up in a loony bin for three years, what need did I have for a bank account?" she snapped.

"I'll take that as a no," Matt said, before turning his attention to the little girl.

"Kayla, I'm sure you're happy to have your mommy back in your life again, right?"

Kayla nodded at the camera.

"Do you miss your daddy?"

Again Kayla nodded.

"If he's watching, is there anything you'd like to say to him?"

For the first time since the interview began, Kayla tore her eyes from the camera and briefly looked at her mother. "It's okay, baby," Denise whispered.

Kayla took a mighty gulp, looked dead into the blooming eye of the camera and said nothing.

Geneva and Crystal shook their heads sadly. "All of this shit is really going to screw that child up," Geneva said as she clicked the television off.

"I think it already has," Crystal sighed.

Crystal still found it hard to believe that she had almost become a polygamist's wife.

"Girl, for being the most pragmatic of us all, you've certainly found yourself in some strange relationships," Geneva commented one day.

Crystal had nodded her head in agreement.

Days later, a hundred grand magically appeared in her bank account. She knew it was from Claude and threatened to give it all away, to donate it to a charity, but Geneva popped her upside the head and asked if she'd lost all the sense God had given her. "You earned that money, girl!"

For some reason Geneva's words made her feel cheap. Like she'd been Claude's personal call girl instead of wife-to-be. She'd loved him, still loved him, and sometimes she cried herself to sleep over him.

Crystal didn't want his money, she wanted an apology, or at the very least an explanation.

Geneva always knew when Crystal was having one of those moments, and when she saw the sadness on her friend's face, she'd wrap her thick arms around Crystal's shoulders and say, "It's going to be all right, girl. God don't ever close a door without opening a window."

Crystal found a sunny two-bedroom apartment just blocks away from Geneva. Geneva was thrilled to pieces that Crystal had decided to remain in Brooklyn.

One day as they sat Indian-style on the floor of the spacious living room looking at paint swatches, Crystal's head suddenly popped up and she asked, "So you still haven't heard from Karma?"

"Nope, her cell phone is disconnected and her landlord said she just up and left one day. No forwarding address or anything. It's like the girl just vanished into thin air."

# 47

It was probably a stupid move on her part. But she had not been in her right mind at the time. Still feeling ashamed and hurt.

But there was no use crying over spilled milk, what was done was done.

Karma had called Lieberman and Lieberman to advise that she would not be returning. She spoke with Arnie, who promptly called her unprofessional.

"Two weeks' notice, Karma, that's what you do!" he'd bellowed. "And don't think for one moment that I'll be giving you a reference!"

Karma flinched at the sound of his phone being slammed down onto its cradle.

Two days later, she swung her front door open to find Joshua standing at its threshold.

"Mr. Lieberman?" she uttered in surprise.

Joshua quickly dropped his eyes and used the toe of one of his expensive leather shoes to kick at something Karma couldn't see.

"I-I was worried about you," he announced, barely above a whisper.

Karma was stunned.

"Oh?"

"Yes," he mumbled as he toyed bashfully with the buttons of his Ralph Lauren shirt.

"Um . . . well . . . that's sweet, I guess. But I'm fine."

They stood in silence for a moment before Joshua raised his head and looked directly into Karma's eyes and asked, "Can I come in?"

She didn't have much in the apartment to eat. He said he wasn't hungry but that he would take a cup of tea.

Their conversation started out bumpy, like an old car traveling over an unpaved road. Karma was still trying to understand exactly why Joshua had decided to travel all the way to Brooklyn, instead of simply picking up the phone and calling her.

When his hand fell on her knee and remained there, it finally became clear to her.

"I want to, to help you in any way I can—" he stammered, the palm of his hand trembling against her skin.

Karma smiled; he was sweet, like a little boy with a crush.

She patted the top of his hand and then removed it from her knee and set it gently down onto his thigh.

He looked at her again. He was biting his lower lip and he looked terribly vulnerable at that moment, and it excited her.

She felt a rush of heat gush between her legs. "You wanna fuck me, Joshua, don't you?"

Joshua's mouth dropped open in surprise.

Karma didn't know why she'd said it. Maybe, she thought as she rose from the couch and started toward the bedroom, she'd said it just to see the look on his face. Or maybe she'd said it and meant it, because she wanted to use someone the way Claude had used her.

Joshua stumbled after her, his erection straining against the khaki material of his pants.

She sat down on the bed and slipped her sweatpants off; the lacey underwear followed. She pulled the T-shirt over her head. She wasn't wearing a bra, and a gurgling sound escaped Joshua's throat when his eyes fell on her magnificent bosom.

"Well?" Karma admonished when Joshua just stood there with a stupefied look on his face.

He undressed in a flash and climbed onto the bed. Karma expected him to treat her body and their sex as some prepubescent boy would. But that thought was quickly banished when he pressed the most gentle kiss she'd ever received onto her lips.

Slowly, rhythmically he moved the palm of his hand over her erect nipples, sending shockwaves of pleasure through her body.

He took excruciating time with her. Nibbling her earlobes, running his tongue down the nape of her neck, her spine, and around her buttocks. He whispered, "I want to taste every inch of you." And he did. He sucked each one of her toes and fingers before burying his tongue in her navel and then finally guiding it down between her legs, where he lapped her wetness up as if it were life-giving water.

Karma grabbed hold of his silky curls and pulled. She'd been squirming with delight when suddenly a lightning bolt shot through her body and her back arched high off the bed. She dug her heels deep into the mattress as her climax raced through her.

She came howling, a sound she was sure she'd never made before.

Joshua didn't give her any time to recover. Her body still twitching with waves of pleasure, he mounted her, slowly pushing his throbbing penis deep into her wetness. Karma whimpered as she wrapped her legs around his back and pushed him deeper.

He mumbled something that sounded like love in her ear. Karma would address that later, she told herself as her body began to climax once again.

Weeks later, in her new apartment, Karma gargled and then spat into the sink. She'd been feeling nauseous for the past two days, and her breasts felt like a ton of bricks.

Supposing her period was on its way, she walked into the kitchen and poured herself a cup of coffee.

Back in the living room, she sat down on the sofa and flicked on the television. Matt Lauer was interviewing Denise Justine. Karma watched with great interest, as she took tiny sips from her mug.

She'd shared the whole sordid tale with Joshua, who had slowly installed himself in her life. He was in love with her, head over heels in love, and wanted more than anything to make her his wife.

Karma was considering it. She had yet to unearth similar feelings for him, but she supposed over time she would learn to love him.

After the interview, the *Today* show sponsors had their say, and then Meredith Vieira smiled into the camera and announced the date and time.

Karma brought the mug back up to her lips, took another sip, and then cocked her head to the side as if she was listening for something.

She set the mug down and slowly brought herself to a standing position.

Suddenly she felt older than her years as she moved into the kitchen and toward the tiny magnet calendar that clung to the refrigerator door.

Karma gasped. She was late. Two weeks late!

Karma closed her eyes and thought back to that fateful night with Claude.

No condom.

Her memory slipped to the first time with Joshua.

Again, no condom.

Karma sunk down to the floor and pressed her fists against her temples in an effort to quiet the voice that was laughing hysterically in her head.

# three months later

isla holbox, mexico

# 48

Maria eased herself daintily down onto the wooden chair the tall, sun-kissed man with the full beard and the smiling eyes pulled out for her.

"Gracias," she said, after he made a big production of unfolding the paper napkin and placing it in her lap.

This was their second date. And already Maria was developing feelings for this handsome gringo.

He'd approached her a few weeks back as she sat reading a Harlequin romance under the tamarind tree in the town square.

Her English was so-so, and his Spanish was much the same, but even with the language barrier, they'd talked for hours.

He said, "You can call me Papi."

He was a gringo on extended holiday, renting a small house on the beach.

"What do you do?" she asked.

"Live life to the fullest," was his response.

She liked that answer.

He told her about all of the places in the world that he'd been and then he said, "I'd like to show you those places one day."

Maria had a traveler's heart, and although she'd never ventured farther than Cancún, she'd experienced the world in the books she read.

Now the man who called himself Papi reached across the table and gently pressed his massive palm against her cheek and said, "Sure, you are beautiful, intelligent and sexy . . ."

Maria's face blushed crimson at the word "sexy."

". . . but are you trustworthy and obedient?"

one year later

# 49

"Hello?"

"May I please speak with Shenelody Miller?"

"This is she."

"Hello, Shenelody, this is Oprah Winfrey."

Silence.

"Shenelody?"

"Yes."

"This is Oprah Winfrey and I—"

"Whoever you are, this ain't fucking funny—"

"No, really, this is Oprah Winfrey, and I just want to let you know that I read your memoir, *Lover Man,* and I LOVED IT!"

"Is this really Oprah?"

"I'd like to make this my November book-club pick."

Silence.

"Shenelody? Shenelody? I think the child done passed out, ya'll. Someone call 911 in Plainfield, New Jersey, please."

# Gratitude

The universe
My family and friends
My editors, Phyllis Grann and Karyn Marcus
Everyone at Broadway Books
My characters: Geneva, Crystal, Noah, Chevy, and Karma, who
    lent light and laughter to my life
And, finally, I'm grateful to you, my readers, for continuously
    supporting my work.

Good things!
Geneva